A TIME TO LOVE

Christina Green

CHIVERS

British Library Cataloguing in Publication Data available

This Large Print edition published by AudioGO Ltd, Bath, 2012.
Published by arrangement with the Author.

U.K. Hardcover   ISBN   978 1 4458 4475 6
U.K. Softcover   ISBN   978 1 4458 4476 3

Printed and bound in Great Britain by
MPG Books Group Limited

'NO-ONE INTERESTING EVER COMES HERE'

Robert Burnham put on his spectacles and opened the letter lying by his plate. 'From your aunt Joanna—I know that spindly writing,' he said, smiling across the breakfast table at the two girls sitting opposite him.

'Not coming to stay, I hope? She's so fussy when she comes here.'

Gemma's face tightened into a frown and her father said sternly, 'That's no way to talk about your aunt when she's so fond of you. Let's see what she has to say.'

Alice turned to look at her younger half-sister. 'If she's inviting us to go and visit, well, you can go, but I certainly shan't.'

'Why ever not? A chance to see the shops and meet people—so much better than living in this dull, quiet village. No-one interesting ever comes here and as for fashion, well . . .' Gemma pouted and dropped her spoon back into the plate of half finished porridge.

Robert Burnham took off his spectacles, replaced the letter in its envelope and looked at them both. 'You're right—your aunt Jo is inviting you and Alice to go and stay for a short visit. She suggests next week. What do you think, girls?'

Alice cracked the top of her boiled egg and

1

said slowly, 'The school term will be finished—of course she knows that, and so I'm included in the invitation. But I'm afraid I shall have to excuse myself.'

Mr Burnham said gently, 'I hope you can explain without hurting her, Alice. She lives a lonely life in London and perhaps a few days of your young company would do her good and not be too much of a trial to you.'

'But Father, the school holidays are the only times I have to get on with my collecting,' said Alice quickly. 'Surely Aunt Jo will be glad enough to have Gemma and not miss me? It's not as if I'm the lively one in the family.'

Gemma giggled. 'That's true. All you think about is those awful village children you help Father teach, and your passion for herbs and folklore. I fear you'll never find a husband, Alice—for goodness' sake, who in this new twentieth century would ever want a bluestocking school marm like you?'

Alice opened her mouth to object, but their father intervened. 'Girls, behave. I dislike all this argument. Gemma, you're fortunate enough to have a keen interest in all the things that Alice can't be bothered with, so let's leave it there. Now, I want you both to write to your aunt and give her your replies. Try and catch the afternoon post, please.'

*   *   *

2

When breakfast was over Alice helped Nellie, the housekeeper, to clear the table while Gemma disappeared upstairs, intent on some important personal project.

Nellie's faded eyes twinkled as she piled the dishes beside the sink. 'Young lady with summat on her mind, I'd say. What is it, the master cutting her dress allowance?'

Alice shook her head. 'Making plans for a visit to town. She'll be making a shopping list, probably.'

They smiled at each other, then Nellie turned back to the dishes.

'Miss Alice, you gets more and more like your thoughtful ma, while young Miss Gemma's the image of her jolly, fun-loving mother. Different as chalk from cheese, you two, you know.'

'Just as well,' smiled Alice, heading for the desk in Father's study and the pad of writing paper kept inside it. 'Wouldn't do for everybody to be the same, would it?'

Nellie bent to the washing up, and her words were for her own ears only. 'That's so, but I know which one's best in my eyes.'

By lunchtime both letters were written, and Alice put them in her jacket pocket when she left the house for her afternoon walk. Her route passed the village post office and she slipped them into the box with a wave to the postmaster as she did so. And then she forgot about Aunt Jo and the impending visit because the wide, mysterious landscape of Dartmoor was opening up all around her as she took the winding lane out of the village, towards Thornton Gate where this particular journey was starting.

In her pocket she had the usual pad of paper and some pencils while in her mind was the hope of finding Mrs Hext at home. She knew the old lady drove the gig into market on Fridays, but today surely she would be there, waiting for her husband to come home from his work. Fred Hext was the Stonely warrener, keeping his rabbits under strict control, and earning a living doing so.

They lived a good step from the village, a rough grassy track through the surrounding moorland showing where the path led. Alice walked across bright green turf, starred here and there with small flowers.

Mauve *sheeps' bit scabious* and tiny yellow *tormentil* caught her eye and she jotted the names down on her pad of paper. Sheep cropped in the distance, and she thought she saw a group of mares and foals foraging beside some outcrop rocks.

A short distance from the Hext homestead she stopped, got out her pad and pencil again, and wrote down the subjects which were ranging around her mind.

Folklore. Herbs. Healing. Wild flowers. Anything remembered from the past. Plants once found here on the moor and old ways

4

of using them as medicines. Stories the old people still talk about. Old gossip, as bright and interesting today as it was fifty years or so ago. So much to be thought about, written down and then, hopefully, sent to a publisher.

She walked on, thoughts roving. Her collection of old customs and even older plant remedies was important to her and she believed a book of them could make popular reading. The gathering of these facts and fancies was —she smiled—as exciting to her as a new gown or a visit to town and the company of new, young people was to Gemma, but Dartmoor was her passion and excitement— this ancient wilderness which had been home to countless people long before this new twentieth century. So many secrets to find— she felt herself prickling with the hope of Mrs Hext telling her something new— or perhaps offering her something old to rediscover.

And then she saw two men walking towards her. Having lived all her life in this small village of Stonely, she knew everybody—yes, that was Thomas Dauntsey, smiling, talking and moving very fast, but who was the man beside him?

Tall and big with dark hair beneath his soft tweed hat. A man with one arm in a sling and walking with a limp. Tom saw her and waved as they approached, both men removing their hats.

5

'Alice! How nice to see you—I suppose you're looking for interesting plants, are you, as usual?' Tom's voice was light and quick and she smiled back, glad of the chance to renew this particular friendship.

She and Gemma had known the Dauntsey family who lived in the next village for a long time, meeting them at Dartmoor festivities, celebrations and family parties.

'Yes, Tom, and I'm on my way to see Mrs Hext—I expect she has some tales to tell.'

'Give her my best wishes, will you? Daniel and I must call on her some time.'

He looked towards his companion. 'Alice, this is my cousin, Daniel, er . . .' He stopped, glanced at his companion who bowed his head, and then continued quickly, 'Daniel Wells, staying with us for a while. Daniel, this is Alice Burnham, who teaches in her father's school in Stonely.'

The big man held out his uninjured hand and said quietly, 'How do you do, Miss Burnham? I'm glad to meet you.' They looked at each other and she wondered why the touch of his cold, strong hand should set new and alarming thoughts spinning in her mind.

How different he was from Tom, who was always smiling, always talking.

This Daniel Wells said little, but there was something in his deep-set eyes and the way he looked at her which made her think that deep down he might have a lot to say, should they

6

ever meet again.

She smiled at him. 'And I am glad to meet you too, Mr Wells.'

'Daniel had an accident in a hansom cab in one of those crowded London streets,' said Tom airily. 'He hurt his leg and his hand, and is staying with us at Churchill House for a bit and we're trying to help him regain his health.' He grinned. 'Which is why we're taking long moorland walks. Nothing like exercise and this wonderful fresh air to make us all feel better.'

So Daniel Wells was a Londoner. Alice wondered what he must think of Dartmoor and its quiet, remote villages where nothing much ever happened. He would probably agree with Gemma that Stonely was the dullest place on earth.

Alice looked at his shadowed eyes and felt a pang of sympathy for someone so obviously out of his element, and she said warmly, 'I'm sure Tom is right, Mr Wells. Dartmoor is a magical place and will help you to feel better. Are you not finding it so?'

He didn't answer at once, but turned his head, taking in the wilderness spreading around them before saying, very quietly, in a low, resonant voice, 'It's certainly beautiful, Miss Burnham, but as yet I have found no magic, although I keep hoping.'

She thought she saw a hint of a smile lifting the firm, straight mouth and said spontaneously, 'Well, it sounds as if you and

7

I are on the track of the same thing, then. I collect folklore and healing plants, and if that isn't magic, then I don't know what is!'

Tom laughed and Daniel's smile grew more evident. Alice felt a surge of pleasure rise inside her and heard unplanned words erupt. 'Perhaps I might join you in one of your walks with Tom when we can all look for something amazing? There are so many mysterious and fascinating places on the moor.'

'That would be delightful. I look forward to it.' He regarded her and nodded. 'Tom, of course, can't come with me every day, as my uncle depends on his help with the estate, so sometimes I walk alone. Your company would be—' he paused and the expression on his lean face softened—'very pleasant. Thank you, Miss Burnham.'

Tom was impatient to get away. 'Come along, Dan, if we're going back along the river we must get a move on. Goodbye, Alice— yes, we must keep up these walks. And don't get too involved in your magical research, will you? Remember how Dartmoor likes to keep its secrets and isn't always kindly disposed to anyone trying to ferret them out. Make sure you avoid the pixies, won't you!' He laughed, pulled at his cousin's arm, and drew him away.

'Goodbye,' Alice said, and again met those thoughtful grey eyes. 'I shall be walking tomorrow, Mr Wells—and hope to see you and Tom. At this same time, perhaps?'

What was she saying? How very forward, but the words seem to have said themselves. And he was smiling again as he bowed slightly, put on his hat and followed Tom, already moving at a good pace down the rough track.

Alice watched them for a moment, trying to adjust her racing thoughts, then she turned and slowly made her way up to the Hext homestead.

She knocked on the door and Mrs Hext, small, plump and with a welcoming smile, opened it. 'Why, Miss Alice—'tis good to see you. Come in. Kettle's singing, I'll make us a cup of tea.'

Before long they were both sitting by the range, with Alice's questions making Mrs Hext venture back into her past.

'Herbs? Why yes, m'dear—they were our medicine. Like using pansies—heart's ease, we did call it—to ease our pains and aches. And my mother made onion wraps for sore throats. And a bread poultice for splinters and thorns. And then there were charms, too. Every village had its white witch who healed in them days.'

She paused, wrinkled up her eyes, and then went on. 'I seem to remember there's a charmer works out at Vitifer mine—a wise man, they call him. Used to do a lot of good. Ah, well. Now they tell me you can buy pills for everything, but I'd always use the old medicines.'

Alice, writing notes, thought she must find

9

out about this charmer. She was encouraging the old woman to tell more, but soon the memories died and she knew she mustn't bother her hostess any longer.

Then, out of the blue, she remembered meeting Tom and his cousin and said spontaneously, 'Mrs Hext. I met Tom Dauntsey and his cousin, a Mr Wells, on the way here. He is recovering from an accident and walks regularly on the moor. Have you seen him?'

'Why yes, he does often pass this way, sometime with Master Tom, other times on his own. A big man, looks strong, but walks with a limp and one arm in a sling. That must be him.'

'Yes,' said Alice, seeing him in her mind's eye. 'We are going to meet and walk together.' She looked at Mrs Hext's lined face and saw an expression of gossipy interest there, which made her add, 'I want to try to help him to get over his wounds.' She added spontaneously, 'And I thought there was a sad look in his eyes ...' Then she stopped, thinking Mrs Hext must wonder what she was talking about, but she was wrong.

'Livin' in London must be proper wearisome,' said the old lady, frowning as she rocked in her chair by the fire. 'All that noise and traffic. I've seen pictures in the newspaper—I wouldn't like to be there.' She poured tea into Alice's empty cup. 'This Mr

10

Somebody needs a bit of Dartmoor magic and health, I wouldn't be surprised.' She gave Alice a big grin, adding, 'And some of they old herbs you write about, maybe. He does look proper handsome —just the chap for a pretty young girl, I'd say.' Her old eyes glinted with amusement and Alice coloured, drank her tea very quickly, finding her thoughts surprising— this was getting out of hand. Whatever could Mrs Hext mean?

Alice reasoned that she had no excuse at all for thinking of Daniel Wells any more—but, oh dear, she would be meeting him tomorrow. And what if Tom was unable to come—could she and Daniel walk out together without setting all the gossips talking? Perhaps it would be wiser to drop a note saying she had forgotten another appointment and make sure her rambles on the moor never crossed with his.

But then an urgent feeling ran through her, bringing unexpected strength and resolution. No. She would be doing nothing wrong. So she put down her empty cup and got to her feet, saying, 'Mrs Hext, thank you very much for talking to me. I mustn't keep you any longer. I expect your husband will be home soon wanting his tea.'

Mrs Hext chuckled. 'That's so. He'll come back with more rabbits; my soul, what I'd give for a juicy joint of beef instead of rabbit, rabbit, rabbit! But there, they make us a living so I'll say no more.' She got up stiffly showed Alice to the door, calling after her, 'Come again, m'dear. You're always welcome and maybe I'll remember more old things.'

Alice turned, waved and then followed the path back towards the village, her thoughts full and working hard. She had some more material for her proposed book, but another image bothered her; that man, Daniel Wells, who was quietly intruding on her thoughts.

There had been something about him, an air of pleasant strength, the look of a man who enjoyed life and offered friendship to all whom he met. His eyes, although for some reason at that moment were shadowed, and hid what she instinctively knew was liveliness. But, thought Alice sternly, there is no reason at all why he should want to be friends with me . . . just a rather plain schoolteacher whose interest lies in the past history and folklore of Dartmoor. Of course, if he should meet Gemma, that would be quite different . . . but there was no likelihood of that happening, so change the subject. Which she did.

She got home, intending to ask her father if he knew of this stranger, but Gemma greeted her as soon as she stepped into the house and took off her coat and hat.

'Honestly, Alice, I don't understand how you can go out looking so shabby and dull. That awful old tweed jacket, and as for that velour hat—you've worn it for as long as I can remember!' She twisted around, saying over her shoulder, 'Father's had a note from Brigadier Dauntsey, inviting us to Tom's coming-of-age party next week.' Dancing away in front of Alice, she led the way into the parlour. 'We must get out our dresses and see that we have something fine to wear. You know what Mrs Dauntsey is like—always dressed so elegantly, and I don't want to look like a poor relation—so perhaps we ought to drive into town tomorrow and make sure we have the right clothes. Ask Father, will you?' She pouted. 'He's sure to say yes if you ask him . . .'

Alice sat down and opened her notebook, merely nodding to her half-sister. 'Yes, all right, later on. I'm busy now.' She wrote down, *find out who the charmer at the mine is,* and then sat there thinking. How could she get to the mine, even if she knew the man's name?

Gemma watched, smile vanishing. 'You and your old notebook—can't you think of anything more exciting?'

Alice paused. The man at the mine vanished from her mind, and Daniel Wells stood there instead. 'Well, yes, I can.' The words rushed out as she saw him so clearly. 'I met a stranger as I went up to the warrener's—Tom Dauntsey's cousin, a Mr Daniel Wells, who is recovering from an accident.' The image grew. He was handsome, even though his face was tense and unsmiling; those grey eyes and long

13

dark lashes and a big, burly body, showing strength and attractive movement, even as he limped. Something about him, she thought unexpectedly. Someone I want to meet again.

*   *   *

Later that afternoon, Mr Burnham listened to Gemma's chatter. 'Yes, of course I've heard about Mr Wells—the village is full of gossip about him. The Brigadier's nephew, hurt when thrown out of his cab when a coal lorry collided with it. He at once saw to the other occupant, a friend of his, and disregarded his own wounds. A brave man, apparently.'

Alice nodded, thinking hard. 'Yes,' she said slowly, 'that sounds very much like what he would have done.'

Gemma looked up from her sewing, eyes full of interest. 'Is he handsome? Is he young? Can we meet him, perhaps?'

'No doubt he's spending time here convalescing,' went on Mr Burnham, picking up his newspaper. 'So that's why he and young Tom are often seen walking on the moor. I see no reason why we should not meet him. You may see him again, perhaps, my dear, as you go about your researches.'

Alice saw Daniel Wells very clearly, as if he were a picture in her mind's eye and hoped they would, indeed, meet again. She felt something strange that she could not explain,

14

but Gemma's hopes and her father's last words brought a new idea rushing into her thoughts.

'Father,' she said, 'could you invite him here, to tea one day? I'm sure that meeting new people would interest him and perhaps make up for the London social life he must be missing.' She paused, avoided Gemma's watchful eyes. 'I thought him very nice, although quiet. I would like to think we might be able to help him recover.'

'You're a good girl, Alice.' Mr Dunham nodded. 'Yes, I'll send a message to the Brigadier inviting Mr Wells to call.'

He thought for a moment. Then—'and I'd better do it soon, if you are both off to town to visit your Aunt Jo shortly.'

Gemma burst in, full of giggles. 'But not for a week or so, first we're going to Tom's coming-of-age party! And Alice, you're going to ask Father a question.' She nodded pointedly and Alice laughed.

'All right then. Father, Gemma thinks we both need new dresses for this party, so please can we drive into town? Tomorrow, perhaps? Can you spare the trap for the morning?'

Mr Burnham's smile deepened even as he shook his head. 'More money! But yes, you're good girls and you deserve a treat. I'll drive you in myself. I have a meeting in town, so you can shop while I'm busy. But there will be a limit to the funds, I warn you! No Paris creations, if you please. You're both pretty enough anyway and don't need too much froth and decoration. And now, can I have my tea in peace without you two pestering me for more favours?'

Quietness descended on the room as Alice poured tea and Gemma spread honey on Nellie's Devonshire splits. Thoughts abounded, and the girls exchanged smiles as they both made plans for the immediate future.

Alice guessed that Gemma's were on the latest dresses in the favourite shop in town, while she was wondering what she would say to Mr Wells next time she saw him— probably tomorrow afternoon. A tiny thrill of excitement stabbed then, and stayed with her for the rest of the evening.

AN UNPLEASANT ENCOUNTER

The town was busy as they drove in next morning and Mr Burnham warned the girls to watch out for rowdy farmers' boys rattling their heavy carts along the crowded road.

'Go straight to your dress shop and then wait for me to come and collect you in about an hour's time,' he told them as he headed for his meeting place further down the street.

As she got out of the trap, Gemma pouted. 'But, Father, I want to go to the haberdashers, too. I need some ribbon.'

Alice pushed her into the entrance of Madame Laparge's little shop in the main street, saying firmly, 'Don't be difficult, Gemma, let's get the dresses sorted out first and then see what time we have. Good morning, Madame.'

The large woman wearing a black gown and a handsomely befeathered hat was welcoming them, holding out her hand and bowing obsequiously. 'Ah, the Misses Burnham—so good to see you, Mademoiselles—and what are you looking for today?'

Gemma took a deep breath, forgot all her crossness and looked around the small salon with its elegantly modelled gowns of every possible material and colour. 'I would like to try on this one, Madame—oh, yes, and that one, too . . .'

It was a good half hour before she had finally decided on her chosen dress. She pouted at Alice. 'I like this one best. Do you think Father would mind that it's just a bit more expensive than that nasty pale pink thing?'

Alice frowned at her and then gave watchful Madame a reassuring smile. 'It's just that pink doesn't suit you, Gemma, nothing wrong with the dress—and yes, I think the pale green poplin with the darker flounces is very becoming. As for Father and the cost . . . well . . .' She turned to Gemma, shaking

17

her head disapprovingly. 'Can't you hold your unthinking tongue for even five minutes?' she muttered quietly.

Another ten minutes and she, too, had chosen her dress.

'Ah, Mademoiselle, but this creamy muslin suits you and your lovely shining hair.' Madame stood beside the long mirror and Alice had to agree that the understated gown, decorated with a pale lemon sash and matching embroidered bands around the neck, on the sleeves and along the flounced hem, was becoming. She smiled at her reflection and was surprised to see the pretty face smiling back. Not bad for a school teacher who usually dressed in plain skirts and high necked blouses, she thought, not to mention Dartmoor walking boots and old velour hats, and then wondered that Gemma was thinking.

But Gemma was impatiently fidgeting by the door as Alice asked for the account to be sent to her father, and received Madame's warm farewell and glowing smile.

And then, as Alice turned towards her, Gemma opened the door and slipped out. 'I shall be there and back before Father comes.'

Alice snatched at her arm, but Gemma was gone, flying down the street and not looking back. Alice gave Madame Laparge a last smile and followed, hoping that their father would be a few minutes late, and thinking how annoying her young half-sister could be.

Suddenly someone stepped in front of her, and she stopped abruptly. 'Peter!'

Peter Fletcher smiled his jolly, rather fixed smile and removed his hat. 'Good morning, Alice. I didn't think I should see you in town. I thought you'd be striding the moor looking for your pixies!'

Alice felt irritation run through her. Peter Fletcher always managed to say something that she thought foolish, and sometimes quite unacceptable. Even when they were both teaching in the village school, he had the knack of irritating her. Now the reference to pixies, which clearly was all he thought about her serious intention of recording the local folklore, was more than annoying, bringing her already aroused thoughts about Gemma into instant sharp speech.

'Don't be so absurd, Peter. And I can't stop, Gemma is waiting for me.' A white lie, but it was enough to allow her to turn away, and then stopping as he put a hand on her arm. She frowned. 'What is it? What do you want, Peter?'

His smile broadened. 'Don't rush off, Alice, I have something interesting to tell you. Something that may help you with your proposed book.'

At once she gave him all her attention. 'Yes?'

'I have a cousin, Jem Fletcher, who works at Vitifer mine.'

Again, 'Yes?' Why couldn't he hurry up? Father would be here at any minute.

'Well, the thing is, Alice, that he's the family charmer. You know—charms warts and ringworm on cattle, stops bleeding, that sort of thing.' He was looking at her very directly, almost, she thought suddenly uncomfortable, as if he saw into her mind.

Instinctively, she took a step backward. 'That sounds amazing, Peter. I didn't know you had a charmer in the family.'

'Never asked me, did you?'

She thought he sounded suddenly cross. 'Always so keen to get away on your own and find out things for yourself Well, I should be very glad to help you, Alice. I could arrange for you to meet Jem and talk to him. Why?' His narrow set, sharp blue eyes widened and gleamed. 'Why, I could borrow a gig from Vic Simmons and drive you out there. Not far—the mine is just opposite the Warren House Inn. We could even have some tea there one afternoon.'

I don't think so, thought Alice at once. *I don't want to be with you for too long—something rather odd about you . . .* And then, but why? He's a schoolteacher, like me—perhaps I should be nicer to him.

So she smiled and said, 'What a pleasant thought, Peter. But I can't decide at the moment—my father is coming to pick us up and I have to find where Gemma has disappeared to. Excuse me, won't you? I must go.' She turned and walked rapidly away, leaving him standing there, watching, as she hurried down the street towards the haberdashers.

And then another surprise as she almost collided with a tall man coming out of a shop and looking, not at the busy pavement, but at what he held in his hand.

'Oh, really!' Alice felt another burst of annoyance. 'Why can't you look where . . .'

She stopped and felt colour surge into her cheeks as dark-lashed grey eyes met hers, and her stomach turned a somersault.

'Miss Burnham, I'm so sorry. Yes, you're right, I wasn't looking where I was going. I do hope I didn't hurt you.' Daniel Wells's voice was very apologetic and she could only smile in reply.

'No, of course not, Mr Wells. I was hurrying.' *To get away from Peter,* whispered a voice inside her head.

'And I was looking at what I've just bought.' The bag he held was bulky, and at once Alice's curiosity took over. She glanced behind him— he had come out of the art shop—what could he have bought there?

'Do show me . . .' She knew it was rude to be so personal, but he at once opened the bag, producing a sketchbook and a collection of pencils and charcoal.

At once she forgot Peter and felt happier.

21

'Do you intend to sketch when you're on the moor, Mr Wells?'

He put the book and the pencils back in the bag and gave her a wry smile. 'I certainly do, Miss Burnham, but at the moment only with my left hand. So the results might be good or bad—we shall have to see.' He paused and the smile grew, easing the tension around his firm mouth.

Alice felt a great surge of warmth spread through her and said spontaneously, 'How exciting! Why you might turn out to be another Constable, perhaps.'

He laughed then, and she thought how good it was to see him relax. The shadows had left his eyes and their silvery light was most appealing. He shook his head, but kept smiling. 'Not likely, I fear. But we shall see.'

Boldly, she asked, 'And will you have your sketchbook with you this afternoon, Mr Wells, when we meet for our walk?'

He nodded and now she missed the smile, for suddenly his lean face was more sober and thoughtful. 'I look forward to it, Miss Burnham. But I'm not sure that you should waste time on a walk with only me for company. For Tom has to go off somewhere with his father and so I shall walk alone. Perhaps it would be better if you accompanied us next time when he can be with us . . . I have no wish to compromise you, you see.'

Disappointment stabbed as Alice realised

she had been looking forward to this afternoon's walk, with Tom or without him. Now it struck her that it was Daniel Wells's company she really looked forward to sharing, and she said firmly, 'I shall be sorry not to see Tom, but I still have to walk, you see, because I must continue the research for my book.'

Grey eyes held hers.

'Your book, Miss Burnham? That sounds very exciting.'

'It's what my family—and Tom, of course—call my collection of old memories.' She felt slightly embarrassed. He mustn't think she was clever enough to write a proper book—after all, this would only be a small record for distribution among the village people and her friends and family.

Then she remembered what that stupid Peter Fletcher had said about pixies and charmers and blushed crimson, not knowing what to say next and panic suddenly struck. She couldn't stay here any longer—what must he be thinking of her? And where was Gemma? Surely Father would be here at any minute . . .

So she took a deep breath, turned away from those alert, all-seeing eyes and muttered, 'Excuse me, Mr Wells, but I must go . . .' and almost ran down the street and into the welcome shelter of the haberdashery shop.

Gemma was all smiles. 'Look at these lovely ribbons—just what I want for my new hat.'

And then, 'Alice, why are you so red? Have you been running away from someone?'

Luckily then there was the sound of hooves stopping in the roadway and their father's voice calling to them. 'So this is where you are—Alice, Gemma, come along, we must be getting home.'

They left the busy town, trotting down the quiet lanes back to Stonely. And it was a relief to let Gemma chatter on to Father about the new dress, how Madame Laparge had admired her slim figure, the bright colour of the new ribbons which would cheer up that dull old hat—well, she had no wish to look like poor Alice, did she?—and on and on . . . while Alice sat there and wretchedly remembered what she had said to Mr Wells, and what he had said to her. And how he had looked at her . . .

That afternoon she argued with herself—should she go out for her usual walk? He had talked about the danger of compromising her and she knew that the village might start gossiping if they knew she met Daniel alone—already she thought of him by his Christian name—and explored the moor with him. But a new surge of strength forced her to think, well, what if they did? Gossip was rife here in the moorland villages, but would only last until the next shock arrived on the cottage doorsteps. And she needed to continue with her research. So she laced up her boots and pinned her hat on very securely, as she told Gemma, 'I shall be back at tea time.'

Gemma looked up from her sewing and grinned mischievously. 'Don't talk to strangers, and mind the pixies don't lead you astray.'

Pixies again. Alice slammed the door behind her and marched down the path, heading for the escape of the moorland which spread beyond her, hazy in the late August sunshine, and full of mystery. In no time she had forgotten the small irritations of the day and was lost to the splendour of the landscape. But, a short distance from Thornton Gate, which was her customary entrance to the moor, she suddenly decided to turn left, heading for the ring of granite stones which stood just beyond the next big tor.

Suddenly she felt ridiculously shy of meeting Daniel Wells, and if he expected her to be on the track leading to the Hext homestead, then he would have to do without her company. She felt confused; she wanted to see him, but something was stopping her from going to meet him.

In this desolate place she was safe, from him, and from possible gossiping villagers. The Dancing Stones, as the villagers called the circle of granite stones, were curiously shaped and when she reached them, she paused before entering the ring.

Her research had already told her that these were probably sacred stones, erected by the early settlers on the moor and perhaps used by them in rituals of some sort.

Whatever their use, they certainly had a magical atmosphere clinging to them, and Alice slowly wandered into the middle of the ring, looking around at each tall stone, her thoughts flying into the past, wishing she could understand the meaning of the circle.

She was drifting in and out of thoughts and dreams, when a voice behind her said, 'Good afternoon, Alice,' and the shock of suddenly being catapulted back into the new 20th century made her turn abruptly.

In that instant, returning to the present moment, she half hoped that Daniel had found her, but the man standing just inside the circle was shorter, plumper and not handsome and charismatic, as Daniel certainly was.

'Peter!' Her voice was full of surprise and disappointment, and she saw the jolly smile fade as he came nearer.

'Alice, I want to apologise for my foolish remark this morning—about the pixies. I fear it annoyed you and I'm sorry. But I know you are interested in my cousin, the charmer, so I thought I would come and find you. After all, it's a lovely day for a walk, and I expect you could do with some company.' He was at her side, smiling in his usually unconcerned fashion and she felt herself tense and step away.

'Well, I am certainly surprised to see you. How did you know I was here? I might have

26

been anywhere.'

'Mrs Hext said she had seen you taking the path in this direction.'

Anger flared. Gossip! Just what she had feared. But now it would happen with Peter, and not Daniel. She could only smile, banish her ill feelings and say resignedly, 'It's kind of you to apologise, Peter. I know pixies and folklore in general aren't your cup of tea, but I'm very interested in them, and especially in your cousin. But for the moment, do you know anything about these stones that I don't know?'

He started strolling around, looking at each one in turn. 'Well, as you know, village tales are that they are supposed to be maidens who were turned into stone because they were dancing on a Sunday. And see that big one there?' He pointed at the largest stone. 'He was the fiddler who played for them.' Turning, he looked back at her and his grin grew. 'Do you know anything else?'

Alice slowly followed him, reaching out to touch each tall stone as she passed it. Was she imagining it or did she feel a sort of tingle from the granite? For a moment she was scared, but then a new feeling came— rather one of safety and friendship and she said, almost to herself, 'I think this circle has been used by the old settlers for all sorts of celebrations and festivals. I can almost believe the stones are warm.' She looked at Peter.

'You may not believe in pixies, but surely these stones tell you something?'

'Yes.' He was beside her, pale eyes glinting in the sun, his usual smile wide and fixed. 'They tell me we should be dancing! Come on, Alice, let's tread a measure. Give me your hand!' And before she could stop him he grabbed her round the waist and began whirling her around the circle.

Taken aback, Alice could only follow where he led, even although she cried, 'Don't be silly, Peter! Stop it!' But the uneven turf and woody heather stems soon hindered Peter's clumsy feet, and suddenly they were both sprawling on the ground, Peter laughing loudly as he tried to help her up. 'Just a bit of fun,' he said, and then suddenly pulled her close to him. His voice was louder. 'You know how I feel about you, don't you, Alice? I mean, I've grown very fond of you, all the time we've been teaching together . . .' He stopped, still holding her. 'You're lovely, Alice. So lovely.'

Suddenly she was too near him. His pale eyes were wide and staring, his breath touched her cheek and all she knew was that she must get away. 'Leave me alone!' she said sharply, pulling away but feeling his hands growing tighter about her waist.

'Alice, kiss me . . .' She recognised the suddenly harsh note in his voice, and was abruptly reminded of moments when Peter's temper had shocked her. This was how, when he thought he wasn't observed, he had lambasted certain young boys in the village school. Now he was trying to bully her.

She managed to pull back her right arm and aimed a blow at his face, so close to her own.

It was a resounding slap which gave her unexpected pleasure. Peter's surprise loosened his hold on her, enabling her to turn and run out of the circle, down the track, not caring where she went, but simply knowing she must get away.

In the distance she heard his voice calling, 'Alice, come back! I want to talk to you!' But she ran all the faster. She didn't want to have any more to do with Peter, but now she understood the way he was so often at her side, offering up foolish little jokes, asking questions that really needed no answers.

She hadn't thought that perhaps he was fond of her, but Peter's fondness was something she could do without. Looking back over her shoulder as she ran, she saw him following, and tried to run even faster. She must get home and get away from him.

And then, 'Miss Burnham!'

Circling a small outcrop of low stones, she came to a sudden stop. Daniel Wells got to his feet and she saw a sketchbook in his uninjured hand, a small haversack at his feet.

'Is anything wrong? You've been running.' There was a note of anxiety in the resonant voice and at once Alice felt her fright receding.

Even if Peter caught her up now, she would be safe. Daniel would see that she was safe.

'I—I was in a hurry to get home.' Her breathless voice sounded almost childish and she wished she had more control of herself. She needed an excuse—rapidly and without proper thought, she added, 'Being alone on the moor is sometimes a bit frightening—when the mist comes down . . .'

He looked about them and a quizzical expression touched his face. 'Not today, though —the sunshine is brilliant and the landscape is clear.'

Then he raised his head as Peter reached them, and put his hand on her shoulder. 'You were not alone?' His voice was quiet, but his eyes had narrowed.

It was a loaded question, and she realised she must explain as well as she could. 'No, Peter was with me.'

The two men looked at each other and she said quickly, 'Mr Wells, this is my teaching colleague, Peter Fletcher. Peter, Mr Wells is Tom Dauntsey's cousin.'

They nodded but neither said anything. Alice thought hard. 'Peter was helping me with stories about the stone circle just beyond the tor—and—and I think the heat was too much for me.' She didn't look at Peter. 'I felt I had to get home very quickly.'

'So you ran.' The grey eyes were alert. 'Yes, I see. Well, in that case, Miss Burnham, don't

30

let's waste any more time. I will accompany you back to Stonely.'

She swallowed the lump in her throat. 'Thank you,' she murmured, hoping Peter would take the hint. But of course he didn't. His voice was as jolly as ever. 'Exactly what I was going to suggest, Alice. No need to bother your friend. I'll see you home.'

Alice's mind spun. The situation was perhaps laughable, but also quite impossible. What could she do? And then she recalled her father saying that he would invite Daniel to call. Words came easily then, and the smile on her face felt relaxed. 'But Mr Wells is coming to tea with us, so it will be no hardship for him to take me home. Thank you, Peter, but we can manage very well.'

She slid a glance at Daniel's face, saw a dark eyebrow lift and thought there was a hint of amusement softening the straight mouth. But his answer was casual. 'Yes, Miss Burnham, and I think we should get straight back to your house. I don't want to set a bad example by making you late for tea.'

The sketchbook was returned to the haversack, which was then slung over one shoulder, and Daniel offered Alice his arm.

'No need to run any more,' he said very quietly, and smiled at her as they began walking down the slope towards the village.

At his side Alice allowed herself to enjoy the warmth of his arm through the tweed jacket.

31

She sensed Peter watching them, and couldn't help smiling at this unexpected turn of events, and then she began wondering what Father and Gemma would say when she arrived home with a stranger who was unknown to both of them.

RESENTMENT BUILDS

'Father, this is Mr Daniel Wells, Tom Dauntsey's cousin. He has come to tea . . .' Alice saw surprise fill her father's face, but, thank goodness, not the shock she had feared.

She hurried on, 'We met when we were both walking—and so I invited him back.'

Turning to Gemma, who sat by the fire doing her needlework, she saw an expression of sly mischief spread over the little cat face and added very quickly, 'Mr Wells, this is my half-sister, Gemma. She prefers sewing to walking,' and then stopped as she saw Gemma's smile beam out.

'Good afternoon, Mr Wells.' Gemma slid the needlework off her lap and rising, offered her hand.

'Good afternoon, Miss Burnham.' He took her hand and bowed over it and Alice watched his answering smile slowly grow, lightening his face.

'You live in London, don't you, Mr Wells?

32

How exciting that must be.' Gemma's curiosity was soon at work and Alice felt suddenly disturbed. Her little sister was very good at making friends and Alice felt she was being left outside the magic circle. Daniel Wells was her friend, and nothing to do with Gemma. But before she could say anything, Mr Burnham came to the rescue.

He removed his spectacles, folded the newspaper he had been reading, rose and bowed to the newcomer. 'Delighted to make your acquaintance, Mr Wells. And I trust your wounds are recovering? Oh yes, the village knows all about your accident and the way you went to the rescue of the poor horse!' But the twinkle in his eye was reassuring, and Daniel, turning away from Gemma, nodded, amusement filling his face.

'Thank you, Mr Burnham, I am slowly getting better. And I suppose gossip has picked up the choicest bits of the accident. But I did nothing other than make sure that neither the cabbie nor my friend was hurt and that the horse was also on its feet. But small communities like to gossip and add bits of information, don't they? We get the same in London, you know.'

Gemma said mischievously, 'And you coming here to tea will certainly give Stonely something to talk about!' She returned to her chair, but left the needlework on the floor.

Alice thought hard. No doubt Peter

Fletcher would spread the fact that Daniel had brought her home and had spent time with the family. What else would he gossip about? Surely not that she had slapped his face? For a moment she wanted to laugh, picturing the village's shocked reactions, and caught Daniel's eye as he sat in the chair Mr Burnham indicated.

'Well, now we're here, we must have some tea,' she said. 'I'll ask Nellie to bring it in.' She left the room, heading for the kitchen, but pausing in the hall to glance at her reflection in the mirror on the coat stand. Her cheeks were still pink, but her eyes shone, and she knew that something had happened today which was making her life more interesting, much more exciting. Not because Peter had tried to kiss her, but because Daniel had brought her home. Had seemed to understand how upset she was, and had shown himself to be a true friend by looking after her.

A friend? Alice took in a huge breath. Young women of her age were supposed to be looking for husbands. Did she feel like that? And then she recalled Gemma's obvious interest in Daniel, remembered too, that Gemma always got what she wanted.

Entering the kitchen, Alice felt all her excitement fade away. She had had no idea that meeting an attractive, handsome man could cause so many complications. A wry voice in her head asked whether sisters always

34

quarrelled over what they wanted, but she pushed it away. She wasn't quarrelling—merely wondering if Daniel found Gemma more attractive than her—and then she smiled. How foolish she was being. Daniel was just a stranger, here on the moor for a short time, after which he would return to London and they would never meet again.

In a quiet voice she asked Nellie to bring in the tea and then slowly returned to the living room, finding, in the quiet, comfortable atmosphere of lighthearted talk, and her family a reassuring warmth.

The table was soon loaded with splits, clotted cream and homemade raspberry jam, and it pleased Alice to see the expression on Daniel's face as he took his place beside her.

She offered to spread jam on his scone, and as she did so, thought he looked less tense, perhaps even glad to be there, sharing a simple meal. She was just about to start telling him about her latest research into herbal remedies, with the possibility of them helping to heal his wounds, when Gemma interrupted.

'Of course you'll be at Tom's party, won't you, Mr Wells? Alice and I have new gowns, and we're so looking forward to it.' She gave him a big smile and her voice took on the little girl wilfulness that always charmed everyone, particularly men. 'Please will you dance with me? I shall have my card, of course, and if you could put your name down for just one dance,

I should so love it. To dance with a wounded hero! Why everyone will be envying me!' And then, before he could reply, she added, 'And do tell us what you do in London, Daniel?'

There was a shocked silence, until Daniel said slowly, 'I keep busy, Gemma.' He paused, and Alice saw the dark eyebrow lift. Then he added, with a straight face, despite the note of amusement in his voice, 'very busy indeed.'

Mr Burnham cleared his throat, gave a warning frown. 'That will do, Gemma, don't ask impertinent questions. And as for dancing, well, Tom's coming-of-age party is a good week away and Mr Wells may well have other plans.' He smiled. 'But we will certainly invite him to join us this Saturday when we go whortling.' He looked at Daniel. 'You know, of course that whorts—or hurts, as the villagers call them—are the little blue berries that grow all over Dartmoor? Well, we have an annual excursion at this time of the year picking them, and would be very pleased if you would care to join us.'

Alice saw Daniel's brief flash of a smile. 'Yes, I know about hurts—we picked them as children.' Then the smile appeared again, warmer and easier. 'All that business of kneeling down to pick them, and those blue fingers when you've finished, not to mention purple mouths! How well I remember. Thank you, Sir, I should like to join you.'

'Good,' said Mr Burnham. 'Farmer

Simmons takes his cart with the rest of the party, but we take the trap to Fernworthy Farm, and if you find it too difficult to climb the ridge you can pick on the lower slopes.'

Suddenly enthusiastic and cheerful, Alice chimed in, 'We always have a lovely day—we take a picnic, and then end the day by calling at Teignhead Farm where Mrs Narracott gives us tea. We need a rest by then before we start the long trek back! I'm so glad that you will come, Mr Wells.'

He turned and smiled warmly. 'Don't you think we know one another well enough for you to call me Daniel?'

She felt colour patch her cheeks, but couldn't resist his smile. 'Thank you, Daniel. And I am Alice and . . .'

But Gemma was asking questions again. 'Daniel, if you know about hurts, then you must know the moor. Do you live near here?'

For once Alice was glad of her half-sister's curiosity. She looked at Daniel, saw his face fill with what she imagined were memories as slowly he said, 'Our family home wasn't far from Churchill House, the Dauntsey home. You see, my parents died of scarlet fever when I was small, and so my uncle took me in to grow up with Tom. But our old house is still there and I hope to find it on one of my walks.'

Alice was intrigued. 'Where is it, Daniel?'

'On the fringe of the moor, just outside Chagford. I daresay it's a ruin now, but I have happy memories of living there as a small child.'

She wanted to question him, to find out about his boyhood and those memories which were bringing such a warm look to his face, but Gemma, who found Dartmoor a boring subject, and not worth bothering with, had other plans. 'Do tell us about London, Daniel. Have you been to the Tower? And the zoo? And do you go to parties in town with all those rich lords and ladies who live in Belgravia?'

Mr Burnham cleared his throat and frowned at her. 'Gemma, when will you learn to curb your curiosity? Mr Wells, Daniel, is here to recover from an accident which must have caused him considerable shock. So do stop chattering. You must give him time to build up his strength, you know.'

Gemma pouted, but Daniel's smile was full of amusement. 'When we're dancing at Tom's party next week, Gemma, ask me again. Hopefully by then I'll have the strength to answer you in full detail!'

Charmed by his words and not displeased to see Gemma flush and curl back in her chair, quickly Alice took the opportunity to return his friendliness by saying, 'You know, herbal remedies will help you get that strength back, Daniel. A tisane of self-heal could work wonders.'

He looked at her with a twinkle in his eyes. 'That sounds quite magical—can you arrange it for me, please, Alice?'

What made her stand up, stretch out her hand and take his, pulling him from the table, out of the room and into the garden? It was a delightful feeling of enthusiasm about the plants, and also the certainty of his interest. Her voice was light as she led him down the flowerbed saying, 'Look, it's that little mauve flower—do you see it? It's called self-heal because ...'

His hand was warm about hers. 'Because of its magic. I understand.'

Alice wondered what was happening to her. 'I'll pick some and then make it into a tea for you.' Her voice was very quiet and she hardly knew what she said because of the way his grey eyes looked at her. 'Come into the kitchen,' she murmured, and then, turning, walked back into the house.

Suddenly it was necessary to think of something else; of giving him help in healing both his leg and his hand. If she did that, surely she would stay in his mind? Even when he returned to London, perhaps he would remember her ... wouldn't he?

Later, with a small bottle of the self-heal remedy in his haversack, along with the sketchbook and pencils, Daniel left Apple Cottage, with Gemma standing at the gate waving him goodbye, and saying, 'Don't forget to come on Saturday, Daniel, will you? I'll help you pick the hurts, you can't possibly do it with

39

one hand, can you?' While Alice stood more circumspectly in the doorway, hoping he would look back before turning the corner.

He did, and she had a warm feeling that, although he looked at both of them, his wave was for her alone.

*   *   *

Alice awoke to happiness, It was mid summer and Dartmoor was a picture of beauty, with the sun bleaching the moor grass until it shone, and the rocky tors sending long shadows down over the yellow gorse and purple heather. It was the day of the hurts picking. She felt unusually excited and dressed quickly, going down to breakfast before Gemma appeared.

She went into the garden, her mind busy, to pick some knitbone and make a poultice for Daniel to wrap around his leg wound. He must be healed. And she must be the one to help him. She concentrated on the drooping, purple blue comfrey flowers with their hairy leaves and hoped that all the old tales about their healing properties were true.

Returning to the living room she found Gemma trying on the new sunbonnet which she had been busily stitching for the last few days. She tied a huge blue ribbon bow under her pretty face. 'How do I look? Will Daniel like it, do you think?'

Alice put the bunch of knitbone into a

glass of water before answering. Then she said sharply, 'And why should Daniel bother to look particularly at you, I wonder? We're going to pick hurts, not talk about fashion.'

Gemma pouted. She sank into her chair and stared at her half-sister. 'Well, he certainly won't bother to look at you—what a dull dress you're wearing.'

'It's one I don't mind getting purple stains on. Not like you in that fussy, delicate cream thing.'

Of course, she was being as childish as Gemma, answering back like that. To make amends, she put her hand on Gemma's shoulder as she passed, and smiled. 'Yes, the sunbonnet suits you and you look lovely. I shall have to wear my old straw hat so I'm sure to get sunburned and horribly red, while you will still look pale and beautiful. Not only Daniel will look at you, but Farmer Simmons as well, I shouldn't be surprised. Now there's a compliment for you!'

They were laughing when Mr Burnham came into the room and the happy mood continued during breakfast and afterwards, as the trap was loaded with the luncheon hamper, some rugs, and baskets for the whortleberries.

Alice wondered anxiously whether Daniel would remember to come—how disappointed she would be if he had forgotten. But no, Tom drove up in a gig, pulling up the cob outside the front door, saying, 'Off you get then, Dan,

41

and I'll collect you later on this afternoon. You'll be glad of a lift home after all that bending and stretching!' He grinned at the girls and then clattered off again.

Gemma hurried to Daniel's side. 'You can sit beside me in the trap. Alice can go in the back with the hamper. Isn't it a lovely day? I'm so glad you're here, Daniel. Is your leg any better? I do hope so.'

Alice saw him nod and smile and then he looked over Gemma's shoulder at her. His grey eyes were warm and his smile grew. 'If anyone's going in the back it'll be me—I'll do the important work, keeping an eye on the hamper as we go. You girls must be in the front.' With chatter and laughter they climbed into their seats, Mr Burnham clicked to the pony and they were off.

Along the road they soon saw Simmons' farm cart lurching and creaking and overtook him with a wave.

But someone else was in the back of the cart, with the two children. Alice looked over her shoulder, frowning. 'I didn't know Peter Fletcher was coming.'

Her father said quietly, 'But he always does. Surely you remember? Any reason why we shouldn't welcome him this year, as usual, my dear?'

'No, of course not I'd just forgotten . . .' and she didn't really want to remember. Seeing him there was a horrid reminder of

42

that unpleasant scene in the Dancing Stones, but she shrugged it off. Peter would probably remain with Vic Simmons and his family while she and Gemma and Daniel picked nearby. She wouldn't have to talk to him and certainly wouldn't look his way.

But as soon as both vehicles drew to a halt close to Fernworthy Farm, Peter and his black and white collie dog, Ruby, walked over to the trap to greet the girls.

'What a day,' he said, smiling, 'and just a bit of cloud to stop us from roasting. Alice, let me carry your basket for you—I know a very good place for picking . . . Ruby, here girl.'

What could she do, but unwillingly hand over her basket and follow him as he led the way to a group of bushes where the sun shone on the tiny purple berries.

Peter's monotonous voice went on. 'Alice, I have some good news for you. I met old Mrs Davy yesterday and she insisted on asking me into her cottage and telling me some of the old tales that you're so interested in. Talk about pixies and whisht hounds and headless riders—well, she's seen all sorts of queer things on the moor. I told her that you would be very keen to hear what she has to say, so we must arrange for me to take you there one day soon.'

Alice stopped picking for a moment, flicked the hair out of her eyes, and tried to sort out her thoughts. She hoped very much that

43

Peter's behaviour in the Dancing Stones was in the past, and that he now wanted just to remain friends. But to go visiting with him? No, she didn't want to do that. She could visit Mrs Davy on her own without any help from him.

Then she remembered what Peter had said about his cousin, the charmer, but that could wait. She could probably ask someone else to take her to the mine and find this Jem Fletcher.

So she said, 'Well, thank you, Peter, but I think I would prefer to go alone,' and hoped he would accept her excuse. But Peter suddenly got to his feet, looked around him and shouted, 'Ruby! Ruby! Where are you?'

Alice got up, too, and put her hand to her head, shading her eyes as she looked across the undulating moorland to try and see the missing dog which had earlier been running around with the Simmons children. She saw Gemma kneeling by a low bush, with Daniel not far away, talking to Mr Burnham who also crouched on the grass with a basket at his side.

'She can't be far,' Alice said, hearing panic rise in Peter's cries.

'It's vipers I'm worried about,' he said sharply, turning and looking in all directions. 'This is the sort of weather when they lie out in the sun and she could easily get bitten. Ruby, Ruby, come here.'

By now the entire party was alert to the

dog's disappearance. Vic Simmons and his wife, Annie, came across to Peter. 'Got a whistle, have you? Dogs hear a whistle more than a voice.'

Peter's voice was distressed. 'No, no, she's a good dog. She'll come when she hears me.'

And then there was a bark, rising into a squeal of high pitched excitement, and Peter ran towards it.

Alice held her breath. She knew vipers lay in the sun and she knew, too, that a bite could be fatal. Why hadn't she brought with her something to treat the dog if it had been bitten? Even a hazel twig would help to banish the snake's venom, the old people said, if you hung it around the dog's neck.

Further away from where they had been picking, Alice saw Daniel suddenly get up, look intently at something behind the gorse bushes close to him, move very fast, and then bend down. She could hardly believe it when he went down on his knees, his injured hand clumsily making an effort to grab Ruby's collar, pulling her back from where she stood silently, staring down at the ground below her paws.

Instantly she understood—a viper was there, close to the dog and Daniel was pulling Ruby away, taking her to safety.

Vic Simmons was soon at Daniel's side. 'I'll get it,' Alice heard him mutter, and then watched him trying to block the snake's escape into the safety of the bushes. But he was disappointed and soon turned back. 'No good, he's gone.'

By now Peter was with Daniel, pulling the dog away from him and anxiously parting its hair to look for telltale puncture marks. Alice reached them as Peter sighed with relief, saying, 'Thank goodness, she hasn't been bitten. But what a close thing . . .' He turned to look at Daniel, and she saw a strange expression cross his face. Not the gratitude she expected, but a look of what she thought was almost certainly resentment, emphasised by a flush of anger.

Daniel nodded reassuringly to him. 'A warning to us all, groping about on the ground in these bushes . . . well, I'm glad the dog's all right.'

Peter said harshly, his voice raised, 'I saw where she was, you didn't need to bother. I was just going to grab her collar but you got there first.'

There was a strange, uncomfortable silence for a moment, and Alice felt her heart beating fast. She sensed that these two men were building bad feelings between them and it was spoiling the day.

Quickly, she said, 'We've been picking for a good two hours—it must be time for the picnic now. Let's put our baskets in the trap, and then find somewhere cool to sit and eat. Come on, Daniel, you can put your basket with ours.' Turning she led the way back to the cart and the trap, and was comforted when she saw the Simmons family unwrapping their dinner baskets and laughing noisily as they did so.

'Get yourself a drink of cider for that rescue of Ruby,' called Vic Simmons, holding up a stone bottle, and Daniel waved back.

'Let me have a bite first and then I'll be glad of it, thanks.'

At last Mr Burnham, Gemma, Alice and Daniel were settled beside a low rock, with the picnic spread out around them. Alice listened to the conversation that flowed, with Gemma's high-pitched laughter and her father's smooth level voice becoming part of the moment. But she remained silent, her thoughts too busy for words to intrude.

For in the drowsy warmth of the afternoon, even with bees foraging in the heather, the nutty fragrance of the gorse surrounding her, and although a lark trilled overhead, worries began to assert themselves, for she felt something vital had happened just now. Slowly and uncomfortably, it came to her that Peter was definitely resentful towards Daniel, and remembering his bullying tactics, a fear came as she wondered what might happen next.

WISE WORDS ARE SPOKEN

'Let's get on,' said Gemma impatiently, once the emptied hamper had been repacked and put into the trap with the baskets of whortleberries. 'Mrs Narracott will be expecting us soon.' Jumping up, she looked at Daniel, still sitting on the ground and drinking Vic Simmon's cider with relish. 'Mrs Narracott's old mother is a witch, she sits in the fireplace and mutters charms.'

Alice snapped, 'Oh, really, Gemma!' but Daniel grinned.

'I can't wait to meet her,' he said, 'I could do with a helpful charm to make me better,' then got up and walked to the cart where the Simmons family were loading their baskets. 'A good brew,' he said to Vic. 'I'll come and see you, if I may, about buying a cask or two.'

'You're welcome, any time.' Vic Simmons smiled. 'I remembers your old home—out to Chagford, ain't it?'

Alice had risen, was listening, suddenly aware of Daniel's expression. He looked different, happier, almost younger, she thought. His face was relaxed, his mouth lifting. She saw him nod to Vic, heard him say, 'That's right. Empty and neglected now, I believe—but I have plans for it.'

'That's good news. Nice old place, pity to let

it go. Move back, will you?'

Daniel, living here on the moor? Alice held her breath waiting for his answer. He took his time before saying slowly, 'I might, but then I might not. Have to see. Everything's a bit of a muddle at the moment.'

Vic Simmons looked at the bandaged hand and nodded. 'Get your hand working again first, maybe.'

'Yes,' said Daniel quickly. 'That's what I need to do.' He turned then and looked at Alice.

'And you're helping me, aren't you? Working some magic on me? Getting my hand strong and ready for work?'

She was moved by the urgency of his voice. 'Of course I am. I don't know about the magic, but I've picked some knitbone, and it's at home, working into a poultice—I'll give it you next time we meet.'

'Tomorrow?' His eager smile charmed her, excited her.

'Why not? Where shall we meet?'

Gone were the old doubts about gossip, for all that mattered now was that Daniel needed her help and wanted to see her again.

'I'll borrow the Churchill House gig—shall I collect you?' he said quickly. 'We could go to Chagford?'

'And see your old home? I'd love that, Daniel.'

He was close to her, so close that she

49

saw her reflection in his silvery eyes, but the moment was spoiled by Gemma calling, 'Come on, you slow coaches. We're going to Teignhead now . . .' and so they both turned back to where Mr Burnham was tethering the cob to a shady rowan tree, and taking his book out of the trap, ready to spend a quiet hour resting. He nodded at Alice and said, 'Off now, are you? Please give Mrs Narracott my regards, and apologise for my absence. Tell her I'm willing, but my legs aren't.'

Already walking up the hill, Gemma looked back and waved as she called, 'We won't be long, Father.' She paused for a moment, then called impatiently, 'Alice, come on, you're so slow.'

Following behind her half-sister, Alice glanced round to where the Simmons family was climbing into the cart, and then heard Peter's voice at her side. 'I can't come any further, Alice, I have letters to write and I must catch the post. We can't all spare time to wander about the moor, you know! But remember about Mrs Davy. I'll arrange a day when we can go and visit her.'

Alice felt herself tense, wishing that he would stop pestering her. And because of the business over Daniel and the dog, she had to accept that her dislike of Peter had grown. Was she being unfair in judging him so harshly, she wondered? But he was still beside her, waiting for an answer.

It was short and to the point. 'Thank you, Peter, but I shall be too busy to see Mrs Davy this week. Perhaps another time. And now we're going on to Teignhead, so goodbye.'

He didn't move, just stood there, and she saw how he glanced at Daniel and frowned.

Something inside her shivered, but she pushed away the feeling and started walking towards Gemma, waiting for them further up the hill.

At her side, Daniel said quietly, 'I hope that doesn't mean you're too busy to come to Chagford with me, Alice?' and she laughed, at once gratefully free of uneasiness.

'I was just putting him off. Peter can be rather insistent with his ideas, and his proposed visits.'

'Yes,' said Daniel, and she wondered at the tone of his voice, suddenly cold and sharp.

They walked on up the heather and gorse-strewn track, the sun hot on their backs, and she became increasingly aware of the slowness of his progress.

His limp was very apparent, and finally she put a hand on his arm, saying gently, 'Let's have a rest, shall we? There's still a long way to go . . .'

He didn't answer at once, but paused and looked at her. 'How good you are, Alice. Not much fun having to stumble along with a disabled man . . .'

The idea was hateful. 'You're not disabled!'

51

she said quickly, 'just waiting for your wound to heal. Would it help if you took my arm?'

His expression instantly told her that this would be a terrible admission of defeat, but then he nodded and said simply, 'Thank you. Yes, it would help.'

She felt the glow of his body heat through his jacket sleeve, and again knew strange and unfamiliar excitement. Then she thought of Peter who, with his arms around her, had made no impression. Being with Daniel was different, so enjoyable, and also opening a new world of sensation within her. As they walked, she thought what a wonderful day this was.

Teignhead Farm came into view the moment they reached the top of the hill. A cooling breeze touched them as they stopped, looking down at the grey stone house standing, like part of the land itself, by the young river Teign which bowled along in front of it, catching the afternoon sun in its dancing waters. Daniel turned, smiled at her and said, 'Would you mind if we stopped again and I tried to draw this?'

'Of course not. We could do with another rest.' She watched as he took his sketchbook and pencils out of the haversack lying on the turf beside him. Her interest grew. Was he an artist, or just an amateur who fancied drawing as a hobby? She would soon know.

He put the book on his lap and picked up a pencil with his uninjured hand, staring down at the house, small and seemingly unimportant in the widespread landscape. Slowly, he drew lines on the blank paper, lines that even more slowly began to take shape. Yes, she saw that was the farm, with trees just behind it, and something which slightly resembled a river flowing past, but she felt intense disappointment. He definitely was no artist— at least, not with his left hand. She told herself firmly that perhaps when his injury was healed the drawing would improve.

But he was turning to her, holding up the unfinished sketch, saying, 'Not very good, is it? Definitely not what the great Mr Constable would consider a picture?' His voice was even, but Alice heard the note of dark self-mockery and wondered at once what was the mystery about Daniel. For instinct told her that there was one, she had felt it from their first meeting when Tom had paused before telling her his name. Was he hiding something that shouldn't be shared? It was an uneasy thought, but then it was quickly overcome and she was eager to comfort him.

'But that's done with your left hand—surely the other one will do better?' And then she coloured, adding quickly, 'Oh Daniel, I didn't mean to criticise you. I'm sorry . . .'

He drew a heavy line through the sketch, closed the book with a snap, and put it, with the pencils, back into the haversack. Clumsily, he got to his feet, offering his hand and pulling her up to stand beside him. 'Don't worry. You're an honest critic and that's all that matters. You were right, of course, the sketch was awful. So let's go down to the river, shall we ? I see Gemma is already there.'

Together they began walking down the hill, feet stumbling over the sungilded moor grass and the flowering heather bushes. She was saddened by the dark brusqueness of his voice, but almost at once he turned and smiled at her.

'Going down is going to be easier than climbing up. Just watch. I'm improving, you see.'

Alice watched as he made a determined effort to cope with the uneven turf and gorse bushes, and as she joined him, she said lightly, 'That's because of the self-heal tea I made you. It's doing you good already! Just wait until you can wrap the knitbone poultice around your leg!'

In reply he reached out, took her hand, and held it as they continued walking down to the farm and Alice felt that the cloudy disappointment of his drawing had passed.

Now the sun was shining again and she felt as if the afternoon was a success, after all.

When they neared the bubbling young river, on its way to the sea from its source far above them in the high moorland, they found Gemma sitting on the stone bridge, her shoes and stockings off, and her feet dabbling in the water.

'Gemma, what on earth . . .' Trust her young sister to do just what she wanted. But Alice smiled, wishing she too, had the impudence to reveal her legs and feel the comforting coolness of the river.

Beside her Daniel laughed. 'Why not dive in altogether, Gemma? At least that would get the purple stains off your mouth.'

Gemma made a face. 'Am I purple? Oh, well, Mrs Narracott will have to put up with my dirty mouth, won't she?'

Daniel was bending down by the water, taking up a handful and wiping his hot face with it. He reached out his hand to Gemma. 'Not if you give me your handkerchief. Hand it over.' He dipped it into the river, then got up and leaned down to wipe her mouth. 'There you are, as clean as anyone could wish.'

Watching this small, intimate act, Alice saw Gemma's bright eyes widen and her face light up as she dried her feet on her petticoat and put her shoes on, and she thought abruptly, all because Daniel noticed her, and felt some of the pleasure of the day fade. But then they were walking up the slope to the farm entrance and Mrs Narracott was standing in her porch, with a welcome smile on her face.

'Here you be then, all hot and tired, I daresay. Kettle's on or there's well water if you wants a cold drink. Come in, come in.'

The farm kitchen was cool and shady, and

as they gratefully sat down around the table, Alice smiled at the old woman who sat in the dark inglenook by the fire. 'Good afternoon, Mrs Spreyton,' she said. 'I hope you are well?'

Ivy Spreyton looked out of rheumy half blind eyes and cackled a laugh. 'As well as maybe,' she said in her old, cracked voice. Then, looking at Alice very intently, she said, 'I know why you're here, maid.'

Mrs Narracott, busy with plates of bread and jam and a dish of clotted cream, said quickly, 'Be quiet, Mother. Miss Burnham's come here to rest and have a bite, not to listen to your old nonsense.'

Awkwardly, Alice said, 'No, I'd be interested to hear what your mother says, Mrs Narracott. She obviously knows I'm collecting memories of herbal remedies and old tales.'

'Well, maybe after your tea. Now, take some cream and put on yer jam.'

Gemma was eating heartily, but listening and watching. She turned to Daniel, beside her, and whispered mischievously, 'She's probably got a charm for Alice to put in her book. I wonder if she'd give me one, too, to help me find a husband.'

Alice heard and coloured, hoping Mrs Narracott wouldn't take offence, but no, her lined face just lifted into a dry smile, and she turned away to refill the huge brown teapot.

Alice looked across the table at Daniel—

how would he reply? He was looking at Gemma, his eyes thoughtful and she wondered if he would rebuke her youthful impudence. But he only said, 'You don't need a charm, my dear. Just keep your eyes open and be your bright self.'

Gemma's pretty face opened into a huge smile. 'I will—oh, thank you, Daniel!'

Alice could stand no more of it. She needed to change the subject, so said to Mrs Narracott, 'My father sends you his regards, but he couldn't face the long climb up the hill.'

Before Mrs Narracott could reply, Ivy Spreyton's faded voice, from behind them said, 'Just as long as you're here, my love, 'tis all that matters. I heard that you're writing a book or some such.'

'Mother!' Mrs Narracott said sharply, but Alice put a hand on her arm, half amused but also half irritated that gossip had found its way right out here, into this remote place.

However, she decided to take advantage of the fact that Mrs Spreyton had heard the little bit of news. 'Perhaps I could have a talk with Mrs Spreyton? She probably knows the names of flowers which were once used as medicines.' Slipping into the ingle, she pulled a chair with her and sat beside the old woman.

'Mrs Spreyton, can you tell me of a plant which will heal a leg wound? I know about knitbone, but perhaps there's something better.'

57

The old woman cackled again and put her veined hand on Alice's arm. 'There's flowers and all sorts of magic on the moor, maid, and if you look you'll find them for yourself.' She stared across the table at Daniel, then turned back to Alice and smiled. 'There's feverfew for the aches in the legs, and sundew for coughs but think about magic, my love. Just remember that—aye, a bit of moorland magic.'

Alice nodded, wondering what she could possibly mean. She knew Daniel had teased her about moorland magic, but magic, the real thing? That was what so-called witches used, and of course, some of the wise old women on the moor had always been thought of as witches. But surely not her, a modern young woman? A shiver ran through her and she said quickly, 'Thank you, Mrs Spreyton, I'll remember what you've said. And now—can I bring you another cup of tea?'

Anything to get back to normality, to sit down again at the table half listening to Daniel and Gemma telling Mrs Narracott about picking the hurts and filling the little, cool room with chatter and laughter.

And then the bread and jam and cream had all disappeared, Daniel was scraping back his chair across the flagstoned floor, and Gemma said with a stifled yawn, 'I suppose we must start walking back. Oh, dear I'm so tired.'

Daniel offered his good arm and bowed deeply, his eyes twinkling. 'Allow me, Miss

58

Burnham, to support you on this long and arduous journey ahead.'

Gemma's laughter pealed out, and Mrs Narracott smiled as she stood at the doorway, saying, 'Come again. We're always glad to see you.'

Alice looked back into the kitchen and met Ivy's gaze. 'Thank you, Mrs Spreyton,' she said. 'I'll remember what you've told me.'

But the old woman was beckoning with a thin finger. Alice went closer and bent down to hear what the raspy voice was whispering. 'One more thing, maid—when the gorse blooms, then it's kissing time. That's proper magic. Remember that.'

Something jumped in Alice's mind and spontaneously she smiled. 'Yes, I will. Thank you.'

Turning away, she found Gemma at her side, grinning and whispering, 'Tell me what she said.'

'Later,' said Alice quickly. 'It's time to go now. And how dare you eavesdrop.'

Gemma pouted. 'I was only going to say goodbye to Mrs Spreyton.'

Alice shook her head. She hoped that Gemma had not heard those last words, for she knew, deep inside her, that they were important and that they were meant for her alone. And she knew that sometime in the future, she would not only remember them, but even act on them. Sometime. But not yet.

59

She said a last farewell and thank you to Mrs Narracott, and then followed Gemma and Daniel as they headed down towards the river. Listening to the rush and soft music of the burbling water, she suddenly found that her thoughts had sorted themselves out.

Ivy Spreyton had made her wonder for a dark moment if she was indeed a witch, but she knew otherwise. She was simply a woman who was trying to become wise. And perhaps the magic that the old woman had talked about was just her growing knowledge of herbal remedies, and her love for them.

Love. The word filled her mind and she smiled as she took Daniel's offered hand, helping her to cross the rough stone bridge fording the dancing river. What did she feel for this stranger, this wounded man who so badly needed help? Something she had never experienced before, something wonderful and wild. But something she knew she must keep to herself, for he couldn't possibly feel the same about her, an unsophisticated school teacher with nothing much to say.

And another thing, he would return to London once his leg was healed and his hand ready to work again. So she would be wise to foster just friendly feelings and nothing more. But Gemma—what did Gemma feel?

Then, resolutely, she pushed away all thoughts of worry and smiled at him and saw that his grey eyes were full of something that, despite her intentions, excited her. Her heart started racing.

But Gemma was chattering on. She grinned up at Daniel. 'One day we must go to the Tolmen Stone, just up the river. They say if you climb through the hole you'll be healed of whatever troubles you. I don't think you'll be able to do that, Daniel—you're far too big—but I'll do it for you. What a good idea! We'll take a picnic, shall we?

'One day after Tom's party. Alice can drive the trap, she's not a bad driver, and we can leave it at Berrydown and then walk up through Scorhill Circle. I'll help you along, Daniel. And then we'll picnic at the river and I shall take off my shoes and stockings and paddle!'

The words *Tom's party* allowed Alice to ignore the rest of her sister's provocative chatter. She switched her thoughts to it as they slowly climbed the heather-covered hill to the ridge and then, with relief, began the walk down to the waiting trap.

She knew Gemma was full of expectancy about the party and hoped her little sister wouldn't be disappointed. Of course, there were the new dresses, which were exciting in themselves, and she knew that Tom would undoubtedly make sure Gemma had plenty of dances, but what about Daniel? He would be there. Would he be well enough to dance? Slowly she smiled as a picture came to her.

Maybe Daniel would ask her to dance, and she would suggest that perhaps it would be easier for him to sit down and talk—quietly, together.

She knew she was shy of company, preferring always to remain in the background and just listen to what was being discussed. But it would be wonderful to talk to Daniel, their words lost to listeners as the music filled the ballroom and couples chattered and laughed. And a new and exciting thought flashed into her mind.

She knew suddenly that she wanted to be alone with him and then chided herself at the thought. Young girls must always have a chaperone, otherwise gossip would result and, after all, if news of her proposed book had reached remote Teignhead Farm, what else might be carried into the cottages in Stonely village?

Then the picture faded, but a different, more innocent sort of pleasure remained. Putting away all thoughts of the party, she looked around her and was quickly lost in the beauty of the moorland surrounding them, and was at once grateful for her keen interest in all that Dartmoor offered. Mrs Spreyton's words echoed, and she nodded—yes even the mysterious so-called magic that haunted the landscape.

Abruptly the spell broke, as she became aware of Daniel's hand seeking hers. She looked up, met his curious, amused gaze as he asked, 'Where have you gone? You've left me . . .'

'No, no, I haven't, I would never do that . . .' She answered without thought, but with uninhibited feeling and then wondered at what she had said.

'I'm glad,' was all he replied, but his words stayed with her as they walked down the last yards of the track, among mountain ash saplings, and great bushes of gorse. And it was so easy, then, to recall Mrs Spreyton's final words and to wonder if the time would ever come when it was right to repeat them to Daniel.

CHILDHOOD MEMORIES

It was mid morning the next day when Alice heard the gig stopping outside the cottage and footsteps coming up the brick path. She hurried to the front door, giving her reflection a quick glance as she passed the hall mirror.

Yes, she looked tidy and the second-best dark-green linen dress with white braid trimmings suited her. Gemma had already said she shouldn't scrape back her hair so closely, and so now it looped more easily in the nape of her neck, and gave her face a softer look beneath the small, neat straw hat. Yes, she thought happily, I look as pretty as I can manage.

She opened the door to Daniel who smiled at her as he said, 'Good morning, Alice. A fine day for our little trip. But bring a coat, moorland winds are sneaky, you know.'

Why was she so tongue-tied? It wasn't as if she were a young girl—twenty-one next birthday. Telling herself to be more sensible, she stood a little taller and said, with an answering smile, 'Good morning, Daniel. Yes, I'm ready—I'll just get my jacket.'

But as she reached out to unhook the grey woollen jacket hanging beneath the mirror, Gemma came running downstairs, saying excitedly, 'Hello, Daniel, I'm so looking forward to seeing your old home.' She stopped in the doorway, smiling at him, wide-eyed and radiant, and then glanced back at Alice. 'You don't mind me coming, do you? I mean, what would all the old gossips say if they saw you and Daniel driving off alone?' She giggled. 'And besides, I can help with suggestions—I'm good at imagining things. Can we all sit in front with you, Daniel, or should Alice go in the back of the gig?'

In spite of her decision not to let her feelings control her, Alice snapped. 'Really, Gemma, you haven't been invited—and I don't care a hoot about gossip. No, you can't come.'

They stared at each other and Alice realised suddenly how much she envied Gemma's lively manner and her youthful beauty. And then a horrid thought surfaced. Had Daniel actually invited Gemma? Did he want her to be there? But she had thought it was to be a trip with just the two of them together.

Gemma pouted, but Daniel said quickly, 'Of course you must come, and yes, we'll squash up together in the front. It's not far—we won't be too uncomfortable.' He looked at Alice, lifted a dark eyebrow as he gave her a reassuring smile and added, laughing, 'Let's just hope the gossips are taking a day off, shall we?'

And then they climbed into the gig, Gemma taking up too much room, pushing herself as close to Daniel as she could, and almost edging Alice off the seat. But soon everything settled down and Alice realised how childishly she had behaved.

The pony trotted rhythmically along the narrow, meandering lanes. The high hedges were starred with late summer flowers, and the smell of harvesting in the nearby fields soothed her disturbed thoughts. Life was good. Daniel had sounded happy. In her bag she had the knitbone poultice which she would give him when they dismounted, and the sun shone. What could go wrong?

And then, as if called up by her thoughts, Peter Fletcher appeared in the lane ahead of them, walking back towards the village, with Ruby at heel. He stopped as the gig passed, waved and smiled at Alice. 'Don't forget about

Mrs Davy,' he shouted but she didn't reply, just sucked in a deep breath and kept her eyes on the road ahead.

Gemma looked at her. 'Why are you so rude to Peter? You know he's keen on you—can't you be a bit more polite?'

Alice pursed her lips and wished this conversation wasn't taking place. How foolish Gemma was sometimes. She said briefly, 'Don't be so stupid. He's just a school colleague, that's all.'

'But a friend, surely? I mean, he's arranging visits for you—well, that's a very friendly thing to do, isn't it? He knows how badly you want to hear the old tales and put them in your book. Why must you ignore his help?'

Alice kept silent and Gemma heaved a sigh. 'Honestly, you'll never find a husband the way you go on, Alice. You should encourage him. He's not bad looking, I suppose, and he would make a good husband; he's a teacher like you, with his own little cottage in the village.'

Suddenly Daniel laughed and both girls stared at him in surprise. He twitched the pony's reins and said, still chuckling, 'Gemma, you'll soon be setting up as a match-maker, I can see. Why don't you choose Peter for yourself, if he's such a promising chap?'

Gemma pulled herself up very straight. 'Because I have dreams of someone much nicer than him.' She turned, looked at Daniel and gave him a radiant smile and Alice,

66

beside her, was left in no doubt as to her exact meaning. They drove on in silence, for there seemed no more to say on the subject.

It was a relief to Alice when they reached Chagford and drove through the village with Gemma looking at the shops, and on into the narrow, winding lanes leading up to the surrounding moorland.

Alice had a feeling that this visit was taking Daniel into the past, and she sat quietly as, before long, he guided the pony into an even narrower, more bumpy lane, and then turned into a weedy drive, approached by open and rusty iron gates. Alice was surprised. She had imagined that they were coming to find a cottage, but as the pony continued on up the rough graveled drive, she looked ahead and saw, behind the overgrown bushes and shrubs, a large, rambling stone house.

Daniel halted the gig and looked at her. 'Here we are,' he said, and she thought the expression on his face was intriguing. She interpreted it as being glad to have come, but there was doubt there, too and suddenly she understood that this was an important moment for him.

He tethered the pony to a nearby tree, and helped both Alice and Gemma to dismount from the gig, saying, 'I know it's neglected, but it's still a beautiful house, don't you think?'

Gemma said quickly, twisting up her face in distaste, 'I suppose so—but look at all the

67

moss, and the damp, and oh, the smell! Did you really live here, Daniel? It must have been a long time ago.'

He led them up the crumbling steps that led to the front door, which was wedged half open. 'I was here about twenty years.' He paused, looking into the dark, shadowy room ahead of them. 'A lifetime, actually. I was a young boy then. And now I'm a man with memories.'

Alice heard the pain in his voice and knew emotions were being pushed away. How could she help him? She said quietly, 'But you said you have plans, Daniel—plans to make this old place a home again and I can see that it would be lovely, restored and cleaned up. Can we go inside?'

He looked at her and she saw him smiling wryly. 'Of course we can. Bless you, Alice, for your understanding. Yes, I do plan to make this old house liveable again. I wasn't sure, but coming here today, seeing it in such a neglected state, has made up my mind for me. I don't know how I shall do it with this leg and useless hand, but somehow I will. Now look where you're treading, and don't touch anything. I'll go first and make sure it's safe to go in.'

Slowly, stepping carefully and looking all around, they made an inspection of the house. Many of the rooms held scarred and warped pieces of mouldy furniture, some carpets remained, wet and faded and covered with

68

litter, but Alice realised what a beautiful home it had once been.

The kitchen was big and she could so easily visualise the cook and the servants preparing meals for Daniel's family, who must have eaten in the dining room that showed a view of the wild and untidy garden with moorland rising behind it. The drawing room was large and airy, with tall windows and an elegant fireplace, now full of twigs and leaves and dirt.

But it was the upstairs rooms that spoke to her more clearly, in particular the old nursery, with its plain, much-used table, hard chairs and ancient, worm-eaten rocking horse looking out of the uncurtained window into the moor beyond. She turned to Daniel, standing in the doorway and said, 'Did you ride him when you were young? He looks like an old friend.'

To her delight Daniel came over and stroked the dusty horse's wispy mane, smiling as he said, 'I did. And so did Daisy when she came to tea. We argued about taking turns . . . she usually won.'

He looked suddenly younger, and Alice was glad. But then she began wondering and asked spontaneously, 'Who was Daisy?'

Daniel looked around at her, still smiling. 'Daisy Moreton. She lived in the vicarage in Chagford, and used to come to tea very often. We were good friends. I missed her when my parents died, and I was sent to live with my uncle Dauntsey.'

Alice straightened her shoulders and pushed suddenly painful thoughts away. Of course he had friends. He had lived a life unknown to her. She had only known him for a few weeks, but she couldn't stop herself asking, 'And do you still know her? Daisy?'

'Yes. Strangely—luckily—I met her in London last year. We picked up our friendship very quickly. She's a lovely girl, with a generous spirit.'

Mischievously, Gemma sang, *'Daisy, Daisy, give me your answer, do!* Is she beautiful, Daniel?'

He turned away from the window and Chuckled. 'You and your romantic thoughts—yes, Gemma, Daisy is quite lovely. As pretty as a picture.'

Alice heard his voice slow, saw his smile fade, and wondered wretchedly how much he felt for this paragon of beauties, up there in London. To break away from her thoughts, she said quickly, 'I'm sure she's looking forward to seeing you again when you're better, Daniel,' and then realised the truth of the words. Daniel would be going back to London once he could walk and use his right hand. Away from Dartmoor. Back to Daisy?

Perhaps he heard the tension in her voice and wondered what she was feeling. He said, more cheerfully, 'Well, we've seen enough indoors. Let's explore the garden, shall we? Careful how you go down those uneven stairs,

Gemma.'

Outside in the sudden eye-blinking sunshine, they wandered through forgotten paths, finding wild flowers and weeds had overgrown what had probably once been formal borders full of stately bedding plants, and almost losing themselves in the bushy wilderness covering the remainder of the garden space.

And then Gemma decided she was bored.

'Can we go inside?' she asked petulantly as they returned to the house.

Alice frowned. 'Be patient for a little longer, Gemma. Daniel probably wants to have a really good look at things and decide what needs doing.'

'But we've been all over the house!' She swung round, her face cross and her voice sharp. 'Oh, I'm not going to wait. I shall walk back to the village and look at the shops.' Turning away she headed for the drive, calling back over her shoulder, 'You can collect me when you do decide to come away. I shall be somewhere around the market. But don't be too long, will you?'

'Gemma, come back!' Alice sighed as her sister disappeared through the gates. She turned to Daniel. 'I'm sorry. She's always so impatient, only thinking of herself. And so rude.'

He smiled. 'Don't worry. She's very young, she wants life, not to waste time in an ancient, mouldering house. Perhaps we should leave, too?'

'I don't think you're ready to do so, not yet, are you?' Alice sensed his need to stay and realised that perhaps this time of memories might be healing.

Brushing aside twigs and dust, she sat down on a garden seat which was almost covered by a fragrant white rose which had spread itself wildly in every direction. 'I'll stay here while you do what you want.' She smiled up at him and was rewarded with a smile that warmed his lean face.

He leaned down and touched her hand. 'Alice, you seem to be able to read my mind. It must be that old Dartmoor magic you talked about.'

They laughed and she felt a new ease spreading through her. Yes, perhaps she had read his mind—but it wasn't magic, her thoughts told her. It was something more real. It was a growing feeling of . . . Quickly she pushed away the all-important word but it insisted on lingering in her mind.

Love. She sighed. Well, even if he had left his heart behind in London with Daisy Moreton, at least they were here together in this evocative house, his old home, and he was looking relaxed and even excited as new plans took hold of his busy and creative mind.

Happily, she sat there for some ten minutes while he disappeared into the house, eventually coming back with a sheaf of papers in his left hand and a pencil stuck behind his ear. He smiled, and sat down beside her. 'I apologise, I've been so long, but I thought a few sketches would help me decide on what to do first. Look, this is what I think the kitchen needs.'

Alice looked at the paper he handed her and was surprised. This sketch was a great improvement on the one he had made of Teignhead Farm yesterday.

She said, 'Did you use your left hand for this?' and was delighted when he took his injured hand from its sling and held it in front of her, saying, 'No, I tried to use this one, it's stiff and still hurts a bit, but I think it's getting better, don't you?'

'Yes,' she said, and looked into his eyes. They were glowing, silvery and full of something that made her heart race. 'Daniel, I'm so glad,' she said eagerly. 'So you think that my medicine is helping you?'

'It's you who are helping me, Alice.' His voice was low and quiet and he put his recovering hand on hers as it lay in her lap. 'You don't realise how much your friendship—and that of your family, too—has helped me recover from that stupid accident. And . . .' He paused and frowned. 'And of other things which filled my mind. Other worries. You see . . .'

'Yes?' She held her breath, hoping that he

was going to tell her about the mystery which she had sensed when they first met. But no, he stopped short, blinked, and then stood up, looking down at her with a twinkle in his eyes. 'Nothing important. What matters is that we drive back to the village and find Gemma— and hope she hasn't bought up all the shops. Be careful how you walk through the house, Alice. Here, take my hand.'

The feel of his warm hand about hers, and this was the one she had helped heal, she told herself gladly—was reassuring.

When they went through the half open front door and out into the wilderness of the drive and the waiting trap, she remembered something, and said, 'Daniel, I have the knitbone poultice in my bag, will you take it? Strap it around your leg when you get home, and leave it there until tomorrow. It should reduce any swelling and take away the pain.'

She found her bag beneath the seat in the trap and handed him the cloth-wrapped poultice. He took it slowly, looking at it with curious eyes, and then back at her as he put it into his pocket.

Standing beside the trap close to her, he said very quietly, 'How can I ever thank you, Alice, for all that you're doing for me?'

Words came without thought. 'I don't need a reward, Daniel. Just seeing you get better is enough.'

'So I can't give you a present, to show my

74

gratitude?'

His warm expression and his nearness, so close that she could feel his breath on her face, made her tremble. Her voice was uneven as she tried to control the feelings surging up inside her. 'I don't need anything, really I don't It's been my pleasure just to try to . . .'

Suddenly his arms were around her. 'And it's my pleasure, Alice, to at least show you my gratitude.' He kissed her, his lips gentle on hers.

When, at last, he released her, smiling into her astonished face, she was silent as she tried to return to reality. Then the cold fact that they were standing together in the drive, away from the world, and that they had been alone in the old house for quite a long time chilled her mind.

She realised that he was looking at her with a certain amusement. He put an arm around her shoulder. 'Have you never been kissed before, Alice?' he asked softly. 'Am I the first one who has had the great honour of telling you how lovely you are, and how you deserve to be treated with great respect and affection?'

Her mind was swirling and it was hard to bring it back under control, but she breathed deeply and forced herself to remember all that had happened before that wonderful embrace.

And slowly it became easier, and very necessary, to understand that it was only to be expected that a handsome man would want to kiss any girl who encouraged him to think of her with—what was his word—affection.

So she must respond in the same casual way. What could she say? Luckily, Mrs Spreyton's last words came without further thought. With a light laugh she pulled away from his enfolding arm, turned her back on him and climbed into the gig. Thank goodness he couldn't see her face with its betraying flush.

But her voice was steady. 'Don't be so serious, Daniel. I think it's time to remind you of the famous old Dartmoor saying— one of course that I've put into my book of memories—that when the gorse is in bloom, it's kissing time. And you saw all the gorse bushes yesterday, didn't you? So our kiss was only to be expected.'

Not looking at him as she seated herself and tidied her skirt around her legs, she went on brightly, 'Shall we go? I expect Gemma is tired of waiting for us.'

She dared not meet his eyes, but sensed his surprise, and heard it in his suddenly curt voice. 'I see. Well, yes, perhaps that's the best way of looking at things. So please forgive me. It won't happen again. And now, yes we'll go and collect Gemma. Are you comfortable? Ready to go?'

He was untethering the pony and climbing into the gig. She felt him sit beside her, saw the reins collected in both hands and breathed a sigh of relief as they drove slowly down the potholed drive and out into the lane.

Very soon she would be at home again, and Daniel would return to London. And Daisy Moreton.

Alice felt a deep wound twisting inside her, but resisted any self pity. She had been quite happy until Daniel came. Now all she had to do was to pick up the threads of her old life and be happy—as much as she could manage it—again. How difficult life was, but thank goodness she had her collection of memories and remedies to work on. She would put all of her mind into that.

A MEMORABLE DAY

Alice felt the atmosphere chill as they drove down the lane, and wondered helplessly what she could say to ease the situation, but it was Daniel who broke the silence after a short pause. 'Your book—yes, tell me more about it, Alice.' His voice was firm and cool.

At first she stumbled, but then words came more easily as enthusiasm for her work filled her. 'I plan to record lots of the old Dartmoor legends—strange stories like hearing the whisht hounds as they hunt across the moor on a wild night, and all those tales of people seeing the little folk—pixies they call them. And then there are some of the lovely sayings .

. . '

He cut in quickly. 'I know the one about the gorse,' and slid her a sideways smile.

Alice caught her breath, but managed to smile back. 'Yes, and of course I am writing about all the old herbal remedies—like your knitbone poultice, and the self-heal tea. There are so many of them and it will take me a long time before I have enough for a book.'

Daniel drew the trap to a halt as they reached Chagford market. 'Will this book have illustrations?' he asked, looking around for Gemma.

'I haven't thought about that. Yes, that would be appropriate, and very nice, but I have no talent for drawing or painting.' But the idea was new and exciting, and for a moment she forgot everything else

'You could probably find an artist who would be happy to oblige you.' Daniel lifted a hand and waved. 'Ah, there she is. Over here, Gemma, over here.'

Alice put away the thoughts of her book, as her half-sister came across the square, smiling at them and then climbing into the trap, pushing Alice to the edge of the shared seat.

'You've been so long,' she said crossly. 'Whatever have you been doing in that awful old ruin? Well, anyway, I went into all the shops and look what I bought . . .' She fumbled in her reticule and brought out a small fan which she waved about and looked saucily at

Daniel over its rim. 'I found it in a tiny shop full of old things—it isn't new, but it's lovely and I shall use it at Tom's party.'

Alice took the opportunity to allow Gemma to chatter on about her expectations at Churchill House and so the journey back to Stonely was a happy one, and she felt the difficult atmosphere between herself and Daniel had quite dispersed by the time they reached Apple Cottage.

Gemma gave Daniel one of her big smiles. 'Are you coming in to have luncheon with us? I'm sure Father would be glad to see you.'

'Thank you, Gemma,' he said, 'but I must take the trap back to Tom as I know he has plans to use it this afternoon.'

Alice dismounted carefully, ignoring Daniel's offered hand and only when she reached the front door did she look back at him. 'Thank you, Daniel, for taking us to see your old home. It was a most . . . . Abruptly she stopped, remembering his arms about her, his lips on hers, then, knowing her cheeks were red, she managed to finish, 'a most interesting visit.'

Standing by the gate, his hands still holding the bridle, he bowed to her. 'I'm glad you enjoyed it, Alice. I certainly did.' She thought she heard a wry note in his deep voice and wondered wretchedly just what he thought of her behaviour.

But Gemma came to the rescue, pushing

past her and saying, 'Come on, Alice. I'm starving—let's get ready for luncheon.'

She turned back and waved to Daniel. 'Goodbye—we'll see you at Tom's party—or perhaps before, who knows? But if not, make sure you're well enough to dance, won't you?' And then, laughing, she led the way into the house.

*   *   *

For the next few days, Alice kept to her plan and worked at her collection of herbal remedies and flowers and legends. It was pleasant to sit in Apple Cottage garden beneath the shade of an old lilac bush, reading her scribbled notes, amending and adding to them and thinking of the next step towards the completion of the book.

Gemma, of course, had other far more important things to do. She had her second best hat to trim with the new ribbons bought last week. She must try on the gown she would wear to Tom's party and decide just how to dress her hair for the great evening. When all that was completed and life became rather boring again, she ran down into the garden looking at Alice in astonishment.

'You've been sitting here for days, scribbling away—honestly, Alice, I just don't understand you. How can you stay there so quiet, and not talk to anyone?'

'It's easy,' replied her sister dryly. 'I have a brain that prefers to think, and not talk.' And then she relented, smiling at her pretty young sister, tapping her toe on the grass and fiddling with her fair hair, which streamed down her back, catching the midday sunlight. 'Sorry, Gemma, I don't mean to be rude, but my book is as important to me as your fashion ideas are to you.'

They smiled at each other forgivingly then, and Alice added, 'I would be very glad if you would think of a new way to do my hair for the party. You're clever with these things and I know I would probably just mess it up as usual.'

The atmosphere lightened and Gemma nodded happily. 'I'll make you look wonderful,' she promised. 'That is, as far as I can . . .'

Alice concealed her mirth and started packing up her notes and pencils. 'Time for luncheon, I think, and then I shall go for a walk. Why don't you come, Gemma?'

'What, walk on the moor in this awful heat? What's the point? I can't think of anything worse. No, I have some sewing to do.'

And then there was the sound of hooves clip-clopping to a stop outside the house, and running around into the front garden, Gemma saw Tom Dauntsey and Daniel Wells dismounting from the governess cart which had halted just outside the gate.

'Daniel! Tom! Whatever are you doing here?' she called, smiling welcomingly.

Both men removed their hats and made small bows as they opened the gate and walked into the garden.

Tom grinned. 'We've come to take you and Alice out for a picnic—and I have a mysterious plan for the afternoon. Are you both free?'

By now Alice, too, was in the garden, wondering who were the unexpected guests. She saw Daniel smiling at her and instantly felt all her courageous thoughts about forgetting him fade into the blue. How could she not respond to his greeting? And to Tom's invitation?

'You want us to come with you—what, now? But it's time for luncheon . . .'

'Forget it! There's a couple of hampers filled with delicacies under the seat. And Daniel insisted on bringing a bottle of wine— come on, be brave, Alice—let's eat *al fresco!* And guess where I'm taking you?'

Gemma was wide-eyed. 'Where? Oh, where? Do tell?'

Tom leaned against the closed gate and grinned at her. 'You informed Daniel that he must climb through the Tolmen Stone in order to get healed, so that's what we're going to do. Now, go and put on some sensible shoes, Gemma, and a shady hat, and Alice, you do the same. I'll go and see your father and ask his permission to steal his girls from him for the afternoon. I'm sure he'll agree—after all, Daniel will be there as our chaperone!'

Twenty minutes later, with Mr Burnham's approval, they were off. The governess cart carried the four of them quite comfortably— Gemma sitting beside Tom, who drove, and Daniel and Alice looking at each other from opposite sides of the back of the conveyance where they sat on picnic rugs. Beneath each seat lay a large hamper, and on the floor between them a basket containing a bottle and some well wrapped glasses.

The drive to Chagford, and then on to Gidleigh hamlet, took a little time, but it soon passed for they were all talking.

Tom insisted on telling Gemma about his last year's visit to Venice. 'All that water, all those gondolas. You would love it, Gemma.' And Alice, with Daniel's encouragement, describing some of the old stories she had written in her book.

He listened soberly and then, when she finished, asked, 'And do you believe all this, Alice? Are there really pixies on the moor? And do they truly lead walkers astray? And as for turning coats inside out to confuse them . . . well, how do you know if it really works?'

Alice thought hard. It was wonderful to have someone to talk to about her work, for Gemma wasn't interested and although their father was glad for her to have such an interesting hobby, she didn't think he seriously thought she might get the book published.

After all, she thought, suddenly disconsolate, young women didn't often have careers, even in these early days of the new century. Particularly in the country marriage was the only career deemed possible. Marriage, having babies, running the house . . . yes, that was a lovely dream, but she knew she needed something else as well. But here she resolutely pushed such thoughts away, and turned back to look into Daniel's seemingly interested grey eyes.

'Well, of course, I don't really know—but it's such a fascinating story, isn't it?' she said warmly, and then added, 'It's good of you to want to know about my stories, Daniel, but I do hope I'm not boring you.'

He was silent for a moment, then a smile lit his eyes. 'You could never bore me, Alice. You're far too alive and interesting for that.' His tone lightened. 'Indeed, I can almost foresee a brilliant future for you—Miss Alice Burnham, famous author and teller of Dartmoor tales. Your photograph will be in all the papers, your book in every bookshop! You will sell thousands of copies and make a million pounds!'

They both laughed then and Alice shook her head. 'I don't want to sell thousands, Daniel. I just want to write a book which a few people in the future will be happy to read and remind them of days gone by.'

'So what do you want, Alice, if it's not fame and fortune? What is your dream of the future, I wonder?' He paused, and then, his voice low and his smile touching her heart, 'Are we good friends enough for me to dare to ask such a personal question?'

She felt herself glowing with pride and happiness. Daniel believed in her! But then as she searched for words, she knew she could never truthfully answer his question. For she knew that she wanted a man—a very special man—to love her, and for them to live together for the rest of their lives, but that was no suitable reply.

Instead, she turned her head aside, staring into the wide expanse of the moorland they were driving through, and then said quietly, 'I am still trying to find the answer to that myself, Daniel, so I can't answer it. Not yet.'

'Not yet,' he repeated in his deep voice, holding her eyes with his own, 'but perhaps, one day?'

She nodded, at a loss to know how to say any more. But he leaned forward and took both her hands in his own, as he said very low and, she sensed, for her ears alone. 'One day? And will you promise to tell me, when you know, Alice?'

'Yes.' It was a promise, made on the spur of the moment, small, but immensely important and binding. Yes, she would tell him, one day, when she was aware in her own secret heart of what she wanted from life. And with whom she longed to spend it. One day.

And then the cob was slowing, straining against the slope of the hilly lane leading to the open moor. Daniel jumped down to ease the strain, and after a moment Alice joined him.

They walked up the lane, eventually halting by a small farmstead where Tom unloaded the governess cart and asked the owner to stable the cob for a couple of hours.

'We're going to the river to perform a magic ritual, to climb through the Tolmen Stone.' He laughed. 'If we're not back by tea time, send a search party out to find us, will you?'

Everyone laughed, but Will North said soberly, 'Never mind about magic, sir, just be careful that the river isn't in flood. 'Tis dangerous at such times.'

Gemma said gaily, 'I do hope it won't flood. I want a swim, or at least a paddle . . . I brought my bathing suit, you know, and a towel!'

And then, the men carrying the hampers, the rugs over their shoulders, and Alice and Gemma taking the laden basket between them, they turned off the lane and walked through flower-strewn green turf, dotted with small granite boulders and shining moor grass, looking ahead of them to where the open moor stretched in misty folds and trees edged the river, whose song grew louder as they drew nearer.

Soon the music of the fast-flowing, noisy water filled the air, and they had to shout to each other to make themselves heard. 'Look,' cried Gemma, pointing to the huge granite boulder at the edge of the riverbank just ahead of them. 'There it is! The famous Tolmen Stone—oh, Daniel.' She whirled around, almost missing her footing, but was luckily caught by Tom's outstretched arm. 'You've got to climb through that hole, you know, but I'm sure you're much too big.'

Behind Tom, Daniel said cheerfully, 'And by the time we've eaten what we've got in the hampers, Gemma, I'll be even bigger so I'll have to commission you to do the job for me. Do you think you can manage it?'

'I'll try!' She ran along the bank and then turned to look at them, following her. 'This is a good spot—shall we stop here? These little rocks can be our chairs. Alice, you can have that one over there. Tom, there's a big one a bit further along and Daniel, you and I can share this long one—put a rug down and then I'll spread out my bathing towel. There!' Seating herself she smiled happily at the others who were trying to find comfortable seats on highly uncomfortable rocks.

But the atmosphere was a happy one and as they ate their picnic—wonderful chicken pies, boiled eggs, salmon sandwiches, small boxes of salad and baskets of fresh fruit picked from the

Dauntsey garden and orchard and they talked without restraint.

From her rock, some feet away, Alice watched Daniel listening to Gemma, saw his warm smile flash out as she chattered on and on, telling him stories of their childhood here on the moor, and of her dreams of living in London and meeting interesting people. 'Everyone here on the moor is so dull . . .' her bright voice said and Alice felt a stab of resentment.

How could Gemma know what country people were really like without getting to know them?

And that made her remember that she must visit Mrs Davy soon and hear some of her old stories about Dartmoor's past. More tales to tell Daniel, perhaps, who had seemed so interested in her book.

Sipping the last dregs of wine from her glass, she looked at him, saw his attention had moved from Gemma, and was now watching her, and she had a rare moment of pleasure as she realised that even her sister's lively chatter hadn't made him forget that she was here, too.

But then the name *Daisy Moreton* flashed through her mind and she bowed her head. How foolish to allow herself to think more into their brief friendship than there could possibly be.

Daniel, after all, in his own words, was a man committed to another woman. A woman whom he had said was beautiful and clever and warm-hearted. So, think of something else . . . carefully putting the glass back into the basket, she got up, and walked towards the others.

'So how are we going to get Daniel through that small hole in the Tolmen Stone, I wonder?' she asked lightly and wondered how her voice could be so steady when emotions raged inside her.

Gemma jumped up, dusted her skirt and said, 'I'm going to do it. Daniel can stand behind and hold me and I'll just put my head through the hole. And he can say something silly, like abracadabra.'

To Alice's surprise, Daniel said at once, 'Thank you for the offer, Gemma, but I think we must be serious about this. And I hope you won't be upset if I suggest that it's Alice who should guide my thoughts through the hole, not you. After all, she's the one who believes in the magic.' He looked at Alice and smiled and her mind became a jumble of hopes and dreams.

But Gemma was very cross. Facing Daniel she frowned, her heart-shaped face suddenly losing its prettiness. 'That's not very nice of you,' she snapped. 'But if that's what you want, well, I'll go and have my swim. I don't care for the silly old stone, anyway. The story is just a load of rubbish.' Turning away she said, over her shoulder, smiling again now, 'I just hope Alice won't get stuck—she's not as slim as I

89

am, you know . . .' and off she went to find her bathing suit and towel and a large alder tree behind which to change.

Daniel lifted a dark eyebrow, as he smiled at Alice. 'Have I hurt her terribly?' he asked and Alice sighed and shook her head. 'Don't worry, she'll have forgotten it all by the time she's put her feet into that freezing water. All right, Daniel, let's see what we can do about the stone, shall we?'

They approached the huge granite boulder, focusing on the hole in it. Daniel was behind Alice as he warned, 'Be very careful. The water's running fast. For goodness' sake don't slip—here, take my hand.'

She did so, watching every step she took through the ferns and heather and willow bushes that lined the bank and felt her thoughts slowly resolving themselves. Daniel's warm, strong hand and the knowledge of being so close to him drove away all the fears and worries. This was a moment to remember for ever—even when Daniel was no longer here, and she was once again just a village school teacher working on her book.

Slowly, anticipating every step, she stretched up to the hole and pushed her right hand into it.

It was larger than she had thought and for a moment she actually wondered if she could possibly squeeze her whole body through it, but common sense prevailed as she looked

90

down from the height of the boulder and saw the river running fiercely below. What if she fell? No, she must play safe, do as Daniel had suggested and let her hand carry his wishes through the magical granite.

Feeling his hand warm over hers, she said over her shoulder, 'Think what you want, Daniel. Don't say it aloud, but just make your wish, for my hand is right there, inside the hole.'

He said nothing, but she felt pressure on the hand he held, and sensed him sending out his wish. And in her own mind she too, made a wish. The moment seemed a precious one and she almost hoped it would go on longer, but then Tom's shout alerted her.

'Gemma! Come back! Don't go into the deep water—there's a current racing out there . . .'

At once Daniel pulled her away from the stone. 'Sounds as if Gemma's in trouble. Quickly, Alice, we must go and help.'

Together they raced along the bank to where Tom was kneeling on a boulder that edged out over the tumultuous water, bending down, stretching his hand out to Gemma, who had been swept from her stance in the shallows and was now in the middle of the river, arms stretching up over her head, face white with fright, and screaming out for help as she felt the current taking her out of her depth.

Terrified, Alice turned to Daniel. 'What can

91

we do?' she began, and then stopped. He had torn off his jacket, kicked off his boots and was already slipping into the water. 'No,' she cried desperately, 'you mustn't, you're not strong enough . . .' but he was gone, arms thrashing through the water, making his way to Gemma, already just a pale blob in the swirling current.

Alice stood, frozen, watching. He would never reach Gemma. How could he? With that sore leg and the hand which still hurt with every movement? His leg was lame, his hand must hurt so much. But now Tom, too, was in the water, and slowly, as she watched, she saw that the two men had reached Gemma, taken her by the arms and were pulling her to shore.

Wildly, she ran to the bank, and helped to bring her half-drowned little sister on to safe ground. Daniel knelt down and turned Gemma on her side, pressing her body to help get rid of the water she had swallowed, while Tom fetched the rugs and wrapped them tightly around her.

It was a nightmare, but it had a happy ending. Soon Gemma was coughing, moving around and trying to sit up. Her hair, sleek and dark with water, lay in ringlets all over her shoulders, and she shivered, but her eyes were bright, and after a minute or two she was able to smile at her rescuers.

'Daniel, you're marvellous,' she stuttered. 'You saved me! I can never thank you enough.'

Alice caught Tom's eye. He was grinning as

he rubbed his hair on one of the picnic cloths and reached for his tweed jacket 'That's all right, Gemma. I've got a funny feeling—a very wet one—that I helped too, but please don't bother to thank me. We know Daniel's our local hero—first the cab turning over in London and now you in the river. We'll toast him in champagne when we get home, shall we?'

Laughter helped ease the tension they all felt, and by the time Gemma was warm and drier, with Alice helping her to slip back into her clothes, she was strong enough to walk back down to the farmstead where the cob and the governess cart waited for them.

Will North stood by the gate, weatherbeaten face registering no surprise as he saw Gemma's wet hair and assortment of rugs and damp clothes wrapped around her body.

'Fell in, did you?' he grunted. 'Can't play no games with that there old Tolmen Stone, you see. Well, I did warn you.' He sniffed and then allowed himself a tight grin. 'But come in to the fire and get yerself proper dry, maid. Come in and the missus'll get you a hot drink.'

The cottage kitchen was warm and homely, a fire crackling in the hearth and a kettle humming on the top of it. Kindly Mrs North made tea, found a towel to dry Gemma's hair, and radiated motherly care for the next half hour, during which Daniel and Tom were given large horse blankets and told to dry themselves off 'out there in the sun.'

By the time they were all dry and getting over the shock of what could have been a fatal accident, the sky was clouding over and Tom said anxiously, 'Let's get home before the rain comes. It looks stormy and we've had enough water for one day.'

The ride home was a quiet one, each busy with different thoughts, and even Gemma not speaking. Alice's mind was full of the day's events. She felt guilty for not realising that her sister was intending to swim in the river and not just sit on the bank and paddle her legs in the water.

She knew that their father would be upset, and perhaps even angry. Well, they would have to face him and take whatever punishment he decreed—if he thought one necessary. But all that was put aside when she remembered how Daniel had sent his wish through her and through the magic Tolmen Stone.

And then the governess cart drew to a halt outside Apple Cottage and the men dismounted to help both girls get down, opening the gate and accompanying them to the front door, where they looked at each other seriously, awaiting Mr Burnham's reactions to Gemma's wayward behavior and subsequent accident.

Nellie opened the door and her old face fell. 'My soul—what have you all been up to? Miss Gemma, you better go up and make yourself respectable. And Miss Alice, I suspect the master will want to see you —he's in the drawing room.'

She stepped back and opened the door in the hallway, saying, 'Miss Alice is here, sir, and—' pausing while she looked at Tom and Daniel disapprovingly, '—and two gentlemen.'

The little group of untidy and damp picnickers went into the drawing room and Alice caught her breath, for Peter Fletcher was standing beside her father, smiling his fixed smile as he looked her up and down.

A FAREWELL

Mr Burnham frowned. 'Why, Alice—has something happened? You all look rather dishevelled—and where is Gemma?' He put out his hand and she took it, feeling his warmth sending reassurance through her.

'Father.' Her voice was a little unsteady, but she controlled it. 'We went to the Tolmen Stone—you know, on the river—and Gemma paddled, but the water was running very high, and, and . . . she couldn't go on, for the memory suddenly hit her fiercely. But Father must be told. She took a huge breath. 'Gemma was in danger of being swept away, but thank goodness Tom and Daniel rescued her.'

A shocked silence filled the room, and then

abruptly, Tom and Daniel spoke together. 'It was an accident.' Tom looked down and shook his head.

Daniel's voice was contrite, but calm. 'Gemma is unharmed, Mr Burnham. She was only in the water for a few seconds.'

Mr Burnham looked at each of them in turn, but it was Peter who broke the tense silence. 'Good heavens, you must have been mad, both of you—so careless to take the girls there. It's a remote spot, and with flash floods anything could have happened. I think you should be . . .'

But Mr Burnham's stern voice cut in. 'Thank you, Peter. You can be assured I will deal with this. And perhaps it's time for you to go. We have finished our talk about next term's schooling—and the other matter.'

He nodded curtly and Peter said weakly, 'Yes, very well, Mr Burnham, but . . .' and then walked to the door, staring at Daniel with glaring blue eyes, and then, reluctantly, Alice thought, leaving the room.

She heard the front door close and his footsteps retreating down the path then slowly let out her held breath and felt a little happier.

'Well,' said Mr Burnham, in a slightly warmer voice, 'perhaps we should all sit down and discuss what has happened. I imagine that Gemma is drying off.' His dark eyes held a hint of amusement. 'And I will speak to her later about her wayward behaviour.'

He looked at the two men who sat on the edge of their chairs and then at Alice, close to him. 'I understand that what happened was an accident, and probably mostly Gemma's fault. But I do think that such jaunts should cease from now on. I don't want any more accidents, thank you.'

Tom said, without his usual bright tone, 'I must explain that it was all planned with a view to helping Alice gather more material for her book, sir. And it would be a pity if, from now on, she were unable to go about—although escorted, of course—and find more stories, as I understand her research is proceeding very well. And I—and I'm sure Daniel here—would be very glad to make sure she comes to no harm in future.'

Alice looked at Daniel, who nodded, gave her a brief flash of a smile, and said levelly, 'Indeed, sir, you have my word for it. I will most certainly care for her if we go on any more walks.'

Mr Burnham sat back in his chair deep in thought, and Alice felt her spirits rise. Surely he would allow the two men—or even Daniel on his own—to accompany her on any more walks to legendary places or when she wished to make visits to more of the old people.

'Thank you both for the offer.' Mr Burnham's voice was less stern and he smiled as he continued, 'But your help won't be needed, for Mr Fletcher—whom you met a few minutes ago, my school deputy and a most reliable person—has already offered to take Alice to meet his cousin, who works at the Vitifer mine. Jem Fletcher is one of the old time healers, and I know Alice would find his conversation most rewarding. So I have agreed that Peter may take her once he has arranged the meeting with his cousin.'

There was silence, both men glancing at each other and then away again. Alice felt her heart drop. So Peter had persuaded her father that he must be her companion in future.

She felt she wanted to jump up and scream and say she distrusted Peter and didn't want him near her, but realised she must be circumspect and not upset either her father or her two friends any more.

So she managed to control her breathing and say, quietly, 'I understand, Father. And I'm sure Tom and Daniel do, too.' She dared to look at them then, saw disappointment on their faces, but resignation as well. So it was easier to get up, force a smile and say, 'I'll ask Gemma to come down, shall I, now she's dry and tidy again? And perhaps Nellie can bring us some tea —our adventure has made us all hungry, I'm sure.'

She was thankful to see her father nod in agreement, saying calmly, 'I will see Gemma on her own—take your friends into the study, Alice, and ask Nellie to serve tea there.'

'Yes, Father.' So poor Gemma was to be

told off on her own, with no loving sister to hold her hand. But Alice, running upstairs to find her, thought wisely that perhaps Gemma had a lesson to learn and this was the time for it.

After tea, the men made their slightly depressed farewells, climbed into the governess cart and departed, leaving Alice at work on her notebook, and Gemma sitting silently, with a sad face, in her usual chair in the drawing room. She looked across at Alice, and said very quietly, 'Have you made any more arrangements to see Tom and Daniel?'

'No,' answered Alice carefully. 'Father thinks it best that Peter accompanies me in future.'

'Oh,' said Gemma, and that was all, but Alice saw from the change of expression that mention of Peter Fletcher brought certain thoughts into her sister's mind and felt a quick irritation. What had Gemma said only the other day about Peter being a good husband for her?

Well, she decided, forcing her mind back to the Tolmen Stone and its magic potential, according to legend, she would take no more research trips for a good long while. Having Peter beside her was just a bad dream.

*   *   *

After all that excitement, Alice found the days

passing very slowly. She sat with her notebook, recording all that she had been told over the last few weeks, and revising some of the older stories.

As Peter had suggested, together with Gemma she visited Mrs Davy who lived at the end of the village and was told stories about pixies being seen by various local people.

'Small little folks, dressed in green with red caps,' the old lady insisted. 'Mischievous things, why, Emmy Jackson down at Hexworthy had one on her kitchen hearth every night, demanding bread and milk. Yes, she had to get rid of one.'

'How did she do that?' Alice wasn't sure she believed all this, but it was a lovely story and she scribbled it down in her notebook.

Mrs Davy puckered up her old eyes and nodded fiercely. 'Told it to go, and he did!'

Back at home, Alice saw how the pages of her notebook were filling, and then came the remembrance of Daniel asking if she would be having illustrations. Suddenly she realised what pictures would do for her book, and then wondered who she could ask to provide them.

When Gemma wandered into the room— slightly subdued these days, after the kindly but firm telling off from her father—to find Alice looking blankly at her notebook, and asked, 'What's wrong? Run out of flowers and stories, have you?'

Alice said slowly, 'No. But I need someone

to illustrate them. I wonder if there's anyone in the village?'

Gemma thought, and then, 'Why not ask Peter Fletcher? He's interested in art, isn't he? He'll be sure to know someone who could do some paintings for you.'

Alice thought very hard. She knew Peter loved art so he probably would have an artist friend somewhere. But going to see him? Oh, dear! Then a brainwave hit her. 'Gemma, you're so good at chatting to people, so please would you go and ask Peter if he knows an artist I could get in touch with?'

Gemma laughed. 'Why not go yourself? Oh, I know—you've taken against him for some reason. Well, all right, next time I'm down his way I'll see if he's at home. Susie, his girl in the kitchen, makes delicious pound cakes—yes, I'll call on him.'

*   *   *

It was a few days later, when both girls were getting excited about Tom Dauntsey's party and talking about the present they had bought him, that Gemma said, 'I forgot to tell you—I saw Peter yesterday. He's going to find someone who will do your pictures. I expect he'll be around to see you soon.' She picked up her sewing and moved across to the window, where she sat down opposite Alice. 'I told him about going to Daniel's old home last week, and he was very interested. He thinks there's something odd about Daniel and he asked what we thought of him.'

Alice looked up. 'What did you say?'

'That we liked him.' Gemma giggled. 'And that you liked him so much that you spent quite a long time with him in the house while I went back to the village. Then I told him about buying my fan, and he said . . .'

Alice's pencil went flying. 'Gemma! You told him that Daniel and I were in the house together while you went off shopping?'

'What's wrong with that? Oh, I suppose you're worried about village gossip.' Gemma grinned as she threaded her needle. 'Don't be silly. How you do worry about things. Now, let's talk about the party, shall we?'

Alice hoped very much that Gemma was right, that she felt uncomfortable about Peter knowing how she and Daniel were alone together, without any real reason to be so. After all, she told herself, life was becoming far more free now that the new century had dawned, and surely a woman could be alone with a man without earning a bad reputation, couldn't she?

Logic told her yes; in a town or city this would happen all the time, but here, in the depths of what was still a primitive part of the country, she knew that most people stuck to the old traditional rules, and she was uneasy in case gossip should grow from the customary mere tittle-tattle to serious discussion of her behaviour. After all, she was a school teacher.

She caught her breath. Just supposing they called her fast? Only too well could she imagine what a dreadful effect this might have on her father and the school.

But thankfully Gemma's chatter distracted her from such gloomy thoughts and soon they were discussing whether the present for Tom—a book about Venice, which he had visited last year—would please him.

'Of course it will,' said Gemma. 'But now I must tell you the idea I have had for dressing your hair for the party—not all scooped back as you always do, but loose and curled, with a comb and a flower setting off your lovely colouring. After all, you must do something drastic—that knot is so terribly old-fashioned.'

Alice nodded meekly. But she knew that however she tried to improve her appearance, Gemma would always outdo her in beauty.

*　　　*　　　*

The day of the party came and by the evening both girls were in a cloud of excitement. Gemma looked a picture in her new gown and preened herself by the pier mirror in their shared bedroom while Alice tried, in vain, to see herself in it. 'Gemma, please let me see how I look.'

Reluctantly Gemma stepped away and

Alice at last saw her own reflection. Yes, she must be honest—and she hoped it wasn't just vanity that told her how well the cream muslin suited her rich hair, but she looked surprisingly different. And the pale lemon bands of embroidery decorating the dress were so lovely—for a moment she found herself hoping that Daniel would find this newly decked out Alice attractive.

After all, she was no longer the girl in the old straw hat and plain dress who wore heavy boots as she walked over the moor. Perhaps he might even compliment her? But then she looked at Gemma and knew that all the evening's compliments would undoubtedly go to her young half-sister, already pink-cheeked with excitement as she tweaked the flounces on her floaty green dress and fiddled with a hairpiece of feathers entwined with coloured beads.

At last Gemma seemed satisfied with her appearance and said, 'I'll do your hair now. Come and sit down over here.'

Alice watched admiringly as Gemma's clever little fingers attached a creamy rose, freshly picked from the front garden, to a tortoiseshell comb and then fixed it into the thick waves of her hair.

Yes, she thought, I really do look different. Wouldn't it be wonderful if Daniel thought so, too. But then the old thoughts stirred and she remembered sadly how she had rejected his embrace at the ruined house. And tonight, surely, he would be looking at other girls, not at her.

And then Nellie's voice came up the stairs. 'Carriage'll be here in ten minutes. Ready, are you?'

Mr Burnham had hired the carriage for the evening, saying that the trap was far too open, draughty and dangerous for his precious girls to travel in when they were going to such a special event.

Down in the hall there was a confusion of gathering up shawls and wraps, but once settled in their seats, with their father sitting opposite them, the girls waited quietly for the big moment to come—for Tom's father, Brigadier Dauntsey, and his wife to welcome them to the party.

Churchill House was aglow with light as the carriage delivered them to the large, porticoed door, where a manservant bowed, took their wraps and then directed them into the salon.

The Brigadier and Mrs Dauntsey welcomed them and Alice felt her hostess's keen eyes taking in all the details of her appearance. Mrs Dauntsey smiled and said, 'You look lovely, Alice, dear. Now, Tom is up in the ballroom, so go and find him. I know he will be looking out for you.'

Then her imperious gaze turned to Gemma, already smiling and expecting the same kind welcome. But it wasn't quite what she was hoping for. 'And this must be little Gemma—why, how you've grown, child. I hardly recognised you.'

Alice saw Gemma's face droop comically and had to turn away to hide her own smile, for she knew Gemma thought herself a young lady these days, no longer the precocious child of not long ago. Again, Alice was suddenly conscious of time passing, and for a moment wondered what lay ahead.

But then she was climbing one of the twin staircases which led up on each side of the spacious marble-floored hall. The carved banisters were decorated with flowers, and the wafted fragrance swept Alice into a kind of dream.

She looked at the paintings of earlier Dauntseys who stared down with critical eyes, feeling herself in awe of the uniforms and luxurious gowns of the family ancestors. But she told herself that at least she had passed Mrs Dauntsey's inspection, and so entered the ballroom with a smile on her face.

'Alice! How good to see you. And how wonderful you look this evening—that dress is a winner.' Tom's hand in hers was warm, and at the unexpected compliment she felt new confidence filling her.

He led her through the already crowded huge room to a row of small tables and gilt chairs behind which an orchestra played softly. Pulling forward a chair, he smiled warmly. 'I must thank you—and Gemma, of course—for the superb book about Venice. Where is Gemma?'

'I think she's still downstairs.' Alice looked over her shoulder, but no Gemma was in view, and suddenly she knew she wanted to speak to Tom about Daniel. 'Can I ask you something, Tom?' she said impetuously, and was relieved to see him sit beside her, face alert and turned towards her.

'Of course, Alice. What is it?'

Difficult on the spur of the moment to put her worries into words, but they came easily and almost without thought. 'There's a mystery about Daniel, isn't there, Tom?'

His face grew solemn and it took a moment for his answer to come. 'Well—yes, I suppose there is, in a way . . .'

Alice felt her heart slowing down, but she had enough courage to say quietly, 'It's about Daisy Moreton, I think. Am I right?'

Tom nodded slowly, obviously uneasy at this unexpected interrogation. 'Yes, Alice, Daisy is part of it—but really, I can't tell you any more . . .' His gaze left her, swinging around to inspect the crowds surrounding them and she realised he was looking for an escape. 'I must go and find Gemma. I expect she's still with your father. Will you be all right here?' Rising, he added, 'I know Daniel will be looking for you—he's somewhere around,' and then disappeared from the room.

Alice sat in her own tight little world of shattered dreams. The pleasure she had felt earlier in the music and the voices of the happy groups of people in the room, was gone and she was left to accept how quiet and empty her own life was.

She wondered now if she would ever step out into a new life which contained other small pleasures than walking on the moor, writing her book and teaching village children. Perhaps it was, after all, what she wanted. But then her thoughts spread out—what, exactly, did she want?

And then the voice that she knew so well and had been longing to hear until Tom's last uneasy revelations, brought her back into the crowded room. 'Alice, I've found you.' Daniel stood before her, bending down to take her hand and to smile into her eyes, eyes which suddenly, despite her unhappy thoughts, now shone as she met his.

'Thank goodness you're here. I don't know any of Tom's friends these days, and I was contemplating a lonely evening, but you're here and so perhaps we can spend the time together. May I sit with you?'

She nodded and as he pulled out a chair beside her, he went on, 'I—' He paused, and his voice deepened. 'I have something to tell you.'

'Yes? What is it, Daniel?' She thought she heard something in the last words that

108

alarmed her, but he was looking at her with such obvious admiration that the fear faded.

'Later. I'll tell you later on. We must enjoy ourselves first. But at this moment I must tell you how beautiful you are.'

She looked down, felt colour patching her cheeks, but knew a wonderful joy spreading through her. 'I'm glad you like my new gown . . .' Foolish words, but the only ones she could think of

'Not just the gown, Alice, although it's certainly delightful. No, it's you—everything that you are—that is beautiful.'

She met his intense gaze and felt a new sense of lightness filling her. What could she say? She smiled, and then brought herself back to reality. 'Thank you, Daniel, but I must say how happy I am to see that your hand is out of its sling—and you're walking so strongly now.'

'Yes, and all due to you and your magic.' His voice was low, his eyes holding hers.

'Not mine, Daniel—the magic is part of the moor. But I'm glad.'

He nodded and then, as the orchestra behind them started playing a Waltz tune, said very formally, but with a twinkle in his eyes, 'Miss Burnham, may I have the pleasure of this dance? Can you bear to run the risk of my stepping on your toes with my newly-restored leg?'

She rose, went happily into his arms and then they were drifting around the floor, mingling with other couples who had also given in to the lure of the music. Alice felt herself grow light and almost airborne—a relaxed, lovely feeling which she knew could never last, but which, at this moment, was all she could possibly want.

The rhythm of the music, the released perfume from many corsages, and the warmth of the room all conspired to add to her pleasure. She saw couples smiling at each other, watched how hands and arms entwined, and was suddenly aware of Daniel's gloved hand warm around her body, and knew what happiness really was. Could it last? Please let it go on . . .

But the orchestra played the last chord and Daniel stood looking at her. 'Shall we sit out the next one, Alice?'

Instantly the magic faded. 'Your leg—is it hurting?' she asked anxiously and let him lead her to the far side of the room, where a long window opened out onto an iron railed terrace, overlooking the moonlit garden below.

'Forget the aches and pains, Alice. It's just that I need to talk to you.'

She leaned against the railing, glad to be out of the heat of the room, and grateful to the breeze that shivered though the trees and gently touched her bare shoulders. 'What is it, Daniel?'

'I'm going back to London. I don't know when I shall be down here again. I need to ask you . .' He stopped, cupped her face in his hands and looked deep into her eyes. 'Will you write to me? Tell me how your book goes. Describe your walks. Bring the moorland peace and quiet into that busy life I have to pick up again, back in the city. Dear Alice, is it too much to ask?'

She thought her heart had stopped beating. Of all things, she had never imagined that this was what he had to tell her. She had hoped—and hoped . . . but he was leaving. He wanted letters, and nothing else.

A deep, heavy sigh breathed through her and the joy of that wonderful dance, the feel of his hands on her back, the knowledge that he admired her, all disappeared, like a puff of smoke blown away by an errant wind.

Then, slowly, reluctantly, her mind returned her to the truth. She was, after all, just Alice Burnham, a schoolteacher in a remote moorland village who thought she had found all she needed, and now was bereft of everything. But he must never know how she had dreamed of him. How she had relived, over and over, that extraordinary sensation of being loved as they kissed. No, love was passing her by, but she still had her pride.

So she stepped away from him, somehow managed to smile normally and said, in her usual clearly controlled voice, 'Of course I'll write to you, Daniel. And when my book is published, you shall have a copy to remind you . . .' It was almost impossible to go on, and her voice was uneven as she struggled. 'Of the moor and its beauty.'

He was looking at her with shadowed eyes and she had a sense that he, too, had lost all sense of their shared pleasure. But he finished the sentence for her, his voice low. 'Its magic. And of yours, too, Alice.'

Her thoughts jostled and whirled. She put a hand on the rail to steady herself, and could say no more. But she thought his mouth, so firm, so straight, so exciting, grew taut, as if there were other things, forbidden things perhaps, which he longed to say but for some reason could not allow himself to do so.

A STOLEN KISS

Gemma suddenly appeared in the open window frame behind them. 'So there you are! I saw you and Daniel dancing. Well now it's my turn, Alice. Daniel wants to dance with me, don't you?' She lifted her lacy fan and smiled enticingly at him over its rim.

For a moment, Daniel was silent. Then he gave Alice an apologetic look before replying, 'Of course, Gemma, how could I possibly refuse such an invitation? But I must warn you that I am still slightly unsteady owing to my poor, wounded leg . . .' One dark eyebrow

112

raised, and Alice bowed her head to hide her smile.

Gemma said sharply, 'You didn't look unsteady when you were dancing with Alice. You looked, well, rather close together and moving like one person.'

'Yes. That's because I was relying on her to give me the strength that my poor aching leg was crying out for.' There was a note of amusement in Daniel's words, and Alice sighed gratefully, knowing that Gemma's mind had been successfully turned away from other disturbing thoughts.

When Daniel offered her his arm, she accepted it and allowed him to lead her back to the small gilt chair, now surrounded by some overdressed elderly ladies. As she sat down, he bent and whispered, 'We mustn't give these eagle-eyed chaperones any chance to gossip, must we? I'll be back very soon.'

Alice watched him lead Gemma onto the floor and whirl her away in a dance that must have severely tested his wounded leg. She sat there, alone with her thoughts, and eventually came to a hard decision. Their dance together had been sheer joy, but she knew, deep down, that she must not see him again. She knew that her longing for him was so strong that it would be fatal to be in his arms once more, even being close and just talking to him was difficult.

So, rising quickly, before he returned,

her final thought strong in her mind, she slipped out of the crowded ballroom and went downstairs into the salon, where her father was sitting amidst his friends, talking and laughing.

Seeing her unsmiling expression, at once he got to his feet and led her to a quiet corner of the room. 'My dear whatever is the matter? You look so pale—so disturbed.'

His fond voice, his worried face, forced her to somehow control her surging emotions. 'Father,' she said at last, 'I feel rather faint—perhaps it's the heat, I don't know. I need to sit down and be quiet.'

He looked at her very intently, holding her hand as she sank down onto a chair. 'You've been dancing? With Daniel?'

She hesitated. Then, 'Yes.' Her voice was dull. She looked into Mr Burnham's eyes and saw suddenly that he knew. Her love for Daniel was understood, 'Father,' she said very quietly, 'I want to go home.'

'And you shall do so, my love. Sit here while I make arrangements. I shan't be long.' He patted her shoulder, gave her a warm smile and then turned away.

She watched him walk into the hall and then chided herself for upsetting his evening, for she knew that he had been enjoying the company of friends not often seen. When he returned a few minutes later she saw, by the expression on his face, that all was well.

'The carriage is being brought around and

114

will take us home. Mrs Dauntsey is kindly sending Gemma back by her own carriage when the evening ends. She understands that you are not well.'

Unevenly, Alice said, 'How kind you are, Father. But I just cannot stay here.'

He drew her hand through his crooked arm, and she rose. 'I understand, Alice. Indeed, I understand more than you think—and this is definitely the best way to act.'

As the carriage rolled down the road, Alice looked apprehensively at him. 'What you just said, Father—you mean that you know I love Daniel?'

He nodded gravely. 'I do. And I understand that, for some reason, you are refusing to acknowledge this.'

Her mind swirled as she turned to him. 'Father, it's not me who is refusing anything, but Daniel. You see, he is returning to London and doesn't expect to come back here. He wants me to write to him . . .' Her voice shook and her father's hand was warm on hers. 'I am to write about the moor, about my book. But nothing else. I feel so—unwanted . . .'

Mr Burnham sighed. 'My poor child. I understand how you must feel.' He paused and then his voice grew a little deeper and slower. 'But, perhaps it's all for the best. I mean, we know nothing of Daniel save that he had an accident in London some weeks ago and now that he is well, he must of course, return there.' He smiled encouragingly. 'My dear, I know you are feeling very unhappy and lost, but do remember, there are other young men whose lives are more open, and perhaps equally attractive.' He cleared his throat. 'I am suggesting other young men who are also more appreciative than Daniel Wells.'

Alice looked at him sharply, suddenly and instinctively understanding his meaning.

She set her teeth. 'Peter Fletcher, my colleague and your deputy at school. Yes, we know him quite well, Father.' The truth was wretchedly plain. 'And you know that he is attracted to me?'

Her father paused before answering. Then his words were slow. 'He has confided in me, indeed, that he does love you. And he is also very eager to improve his position in the school.

'There will come a time, of course, and not too far distant when I shall relinquish my headmaster position and need a new, reliable replacement. And Peter, happily settled in the village, would be an ideal choice.'

'Settled? You mean of course, married.'

Alice's thoughts whirled as fast as the carriage wheels carrying her home. Peter, hoping to marry her. Peter, whom she thought so ordinary and unappealing. And yet common sense, one of her important gifts, told her that all her father had said was true.

If she married Peter she could remain in

the village, living a quiet and fulfilled life and forgetting all the wild moments and subsequent unhappiness of loving Daniel, who clearly had no equal longing for her.

At last, as the carriage came to a creaking halt outside Apple Cottage, she knew the way she must go. Bravely she smiled at her father as he opened the front door and ushered her into the warmth and safety of their home.

'Dear Father, thank you. And I promise to think seriously about all you have said.' She walked towards the staircase and then turned, as his voice followed her.

'How sensible you are, dear child. Now, have a good night's sleep and I'm sure that everything will seem better in the morning. I'll tell Nellie to bring you a hot drink, and warn Gemma when she comes back not to wake you. Goodnight, my love.'

She heard the relief in his voice and was grateful for his love and understanding, but in bed, she stayed awake for a while, thinking about all that had happened that evening. She wasn't sure that, as her father had suggested, things would seem better tomorrow, but with her natural courage returning she knew now with a surge of new strength, that she would renew her old life. And forget Daniel.

But, just before falling asleep, she asked herself the one all important and infinitely disturbing question—can I really do so?

Gemma awoke her early next morning.

117

'Why ever did you come home so early last night? It was such a splendid party. I had lots of dances, three with Daniel and two with Tom and then—the last waltz with someone else . . .'

As she brushed her hair, sitting on the edge of the bed, Gemma smiled dreamily and Alice was caught by the expression on her half-sister's pretty face. It was the sort of expression she herself had seen in the mirror so soon after meeting Daniel. Was it possible that Gemma had met a man she might love?

Carefully, as she propped herself up with pillows, she said, 'I'm sure you enjoyed dancing with Daniel—you looked as if you did. And I know Tom is a good dancer. So what about the last partner you mentioned?'

Gemma still looked dreamy-eyed. 'Richard Westbrook. He's another of Tom's cousins, and a friend of Daniel's, staying near here on holiday.' Her smile grew. 'He said my gown was superb and that I danced like the fairy queen herself, and that he wants to call on Father, and—and . . .' She threw down the hairbrush and smiling, fell into Alice's arms. 'I think I'm in love,' she whispered. 'Now I can forget Daniel and instead just dream about Richard. Oh, how marvellous it all is!'

Alice held her very tightly, suddenly feeling a mixture of pain and happiness. Pain, remembering her own love, and then happiness that little Gemma was experiencing something she knew only too well to be wonderful. Then gently pushing Gemma away from her, Alice said, 'And what else happened at the party? It wasn't all dancing, was it?'

Gemma went to the window seat and pulled back the curtains. 'Of course not, we had wine and some lovely food, and I talked to lots of people. I even made Daniel talk to me!' She turned, looked back at Alice. 'Did you know that he's going back to London because of some sort of very special event? A sort of test, he said. Did he tell you about it?'

Alice felt her courage waning and all her good resolutions beginning to dim. 'No,' she said, 'but I thought he looked worried about something. What else did he say?'

'Oh!' Gemma got up and drifted towards the wardrobe. 'Nothing much. He talked about you, mostly. Said how wonderful you were—I suppose he meant all that old flower healing stuff.'

Alice felt a new warmth seep into her cold body. But she kept control of herself. 'How did you get him to talk so freely?'

Gemma looked at her in amazement. 'I kept asking, of course. He said I had a built-in curiosity—whatever that means—and was a proper little chatterbox, but he smiled and told me about his drawing.'

'His drawing? But he can't draw . . .' Alice recalled the rough lines in the sketchbook.

Gemma opened the wardrobe door. 'I can't

tell you any more. Now, what shall I wear today? I must be sure to look my best just in case Richard calls .. .'

Alice was deep in thought, watching her sister choose a dress. Eventually she said, as casually as she could manage, 'And you have no idea what that event he spoke of could be?'

'No.' Gemma was no longer interested, but now deciding whether to wear a brooch or a necklace. 'I think the brooch looks better, don't you?'

But Alice was trying not to remember Daniel and his attempts at sketching when they were sitting together on the moor. She pushed aside the magical memories of his closeness, of the brilliance of the gorse, and the flashing sunlight on the rippling waters below. And finally, of Mrs Spreyton's last words—'When the gorse is in flower, that's kissing time.'

With a great leap of determination she got out of bed and said briskly, 'We'll be late for breakfast if you keep fussing about what to wear. Hurry up, Gemma, do.'

At breakfast, Mr Burnham took off his spectacles and smiled down the table at his two daughters. 'My dears,' he said, 'I think perhaps this is the time to accept your aunt's invitation to visit her, isn't it? Have you any other plans, either of you?'

Gemma caught Alice's eye, and stirred her porridge urgently. 'I don't really want to go away for a little while, Father. You see, I—I

. . .' she came to a stuttering halt and Alice smiled reassuringly as she tried to help.

'Father, Gemma has made a new friend and is rather hoping he might call in a day or so.'

Mr Burnham looked from one girl to the other and then bowed his head. Alice thought she saw a twinkle of amusement there, but when he spoke his voice was quite sober. 'I see. And what about you, Alice? Have you anything important that is stopping you visiting your aunt shortly?'

She thought hard. There must be something that would keep her here and which would support Gemma's longing to stay at home in case Richard Westbrook should call. And then she thought about the visit to the healer at the Vitifer mine that Peter Fletcher had suggested.

She remembered telling her father last night that she would think seriously about what he had said—and, although the idea was at first chilling, slowly she came to realise that an outing in company with Peter might just help her to remove her feelings of dislike for the poor man.

'So, Father, I thought this would be a good time for me to accept Peter's invitation to go and visit his cousin, who is a healer. Would you allow me to do that?'

Mr Burnham looked at her for a long considering moment and she knew he was aware of the thoughts running through her head. Then he nodded and gave her a warm, loving smile. 'What a good idea, Alice. I most certainly agree with it, but I think Gemma should accompany you. The mine is a hard living, noisy place and you will undoubtedly need female company to support you amongst all those rough miners.'

He looked down the table at his younger daughter and his smile grew. 'And Gemma, if your new friend should call when you are away, I will tell him that you would be glad to see him another day.' He paused, looked up at the ceiling, and then added slowly, 'I remember the name—Westbrook—yes, a good family, and a relative of the Dauntseys. Yes, child, be assured I will welcome your new friend if he should arrive in your absence.'

Alice looked at Gemma and smiled. 'It will only be for an afternoon,' she said reassuringly. 'And you can wear something pretty to give all those poor miners a treat!'

Mr Burnham put his napkin to his mouth and cleared his throat. 'I will make all the necessary arrangements with Peter,' he said, and then pushing aside his empty plate, picked up the folded newspaper. 'And now, my dears, I feel sure you both have plenty to occupy you until the visit is arranged.'

*   *   *

That afternoon Alice decided she needed to go out and try and lose her worries and unhappiness by walking on the moor. The day was cloudy, but still warm, and because clouds misted the top of the nearest hilltop, she put on her jacket. Dartmoor weather, as she well knew, could change in a moment, and it was always wise to be prepared for the worst.

From Thornton Gate she walked up the track, passing by Mrs Hext's cottage to wave at the old woman working in the yard and receiving a warm smile in return. Then she made her way past the Dancing Stones and on down to the river.

The steep-sided valley was already showing drifts of heather in flower and Alice felt her spirits rise as she walked carefully through scrub and gorse towards the stepping stones which crossed the water and led on towards the higher moorland. Thoughts of Gemma and the Tolmen Stone flashed through her mind, but here the river was a small brook, burbling down the hillside and posing no danger.

Such peace and quiet, she thought, such wild beauty, and no-one else here. It was a lonely place, but it had an atmosphere that calmed her as she found a low rock to sit on. Lush ferns leaned into the water and small sandy beaches came and went as the water flowed along.

She took her notebook and pencil out of her pocket and started making notes about the heather and the mountain ash saplings. A lark sang a paean of praise in the wispy sky above and somewhere not too far away a pony nickered. All around her was nature, bleak in the winter, but now, in late summer, warm and welcoming. She smiled at her thoughts and then knew intuitively that she never wanted to leave this wonderful place.

Yes, she and Gemma and Peter would visit the mine and ask Jem Fletcher about his healing gifts. And perhaps her thoughts of Peter would become happier ones . . . and then there was the visit to Aunt Joanne in London to look forward to after that. London, thought Alice, would be busy and noisy.

Aunt Jo would introduce them both to new people, take them on outings and make social calls, filling their days with rush and bustle, conversation, pleasure and noise. And then they would return to this silence and peace. Gemma would want to stay in London and perhaps one day she might even go and live there, but Alice felt that her home would always be here, among these valleys and peaks, in harmony with the wildness of nature.

She told herself she must think more positively about marrying Peter Fletcher. One day he would take over Father's place at school and clearly would have to continue living in the village. And she would share that small cottage by the church with him. She would teach beside him and perhaps in the fullness of time they would have children. Alice's smile faded slowly as she tried to foresee her future, until suddenly a voice called her name.

'Alice!' Daniel's tall figure was in sight, his hand waving at her. Oh, she thought wildly, I can't bear to see him, or to talk to him. Leaping up, she snatched at her hat and notebook and without thinking further, began to run in the opposite direction, up the riverbank.

She wasn't thinking, not looking—the bright green, seemingly innocent, patch of bog was sucking at her ankles before she realised what was happening. Shock stopped her fighting the pull of the green, murky depths. The old name—a featherbed, because it looked so green and comfortable—ran through her churning mind, but once in the clutches of the deceptive greenery, panic rose inside her and instinctively she screamed for help. 'Daniel! Daniel! Help me!'

He was there in a few seconds, warm hands around her, his tall body leaning forward, keeping well out of the bog, but his strength was rescuing her, pulling her out of its deadly clutches. Urgently, he said, 'Alice, hold on to me. I'll get you out. Don't fight —just let go . . .' and she knew a surge of relief and gratitude as, with reluctant sucking noises, the green bog released her and she fell onto the bank, still held by his powerful hands.

He laid her down on the grassy turf a few safe footsteps away from the bog, wrapped his coat around her shivering body. Looking into her wide, shocked eyes, he said gently, 'You're safe, there's nothing to worry about. Just try and breathe deeply.' He wiped her face with his handkerchief and smiled reassuringly.

Alice took a few minutes to realise that she was safe. That he had saved her. Her thoughts whirled and circled, forcing recent memories to return. She loved him, but then her father's words echoed, and she knew she must be sensible.

Slowly she remembered the decision made moments before being trapped in the bog. She and Peter, Daniel and Daisy. Now she pushed herself into a sitting position and smiled weakly at him as he crouched beside her. 'I—I didn't expect to see you. And it was silly of me not to see the bog—I was thinking about something else . . .'

He smiled back, took her hands and began to chafe them into warmth, 'I was worried when I heard you had left the party last night. No-one seemed to know why—and when I called at your home Gemma said you were out here somewhere. So I took the usual path and Mrs Hext at the warren house said she had seen you coming this way.' He stopped, then added very quietly, 'Alice, thank goodness I came in time.'

They looked deep into each other's eyes and Alice felt all her sensible decisions melt away. When he said with a note of concern in his deep voice, 'Your feet must be very wet. Let me take off your boots,' she could only nod and watch as, carefully, his hands' untied the laces of her soaking boots and began rubbing her chilled feet.

Gradually she felt warm again and lost the terrible feeling of panic that had filled her.

'Thank you,' she said unsteadily and reached out to start putting her boots on again. But his hands held hers and he drew her up towards him until her face was close to his. 'Oh, Alice,' he murmured and hungrily kissed her melting lips.

Magic, she thought wildly as sensations of pleasure and happiness swept through her. And then the black cloud returned. Moorland magic, but it can't last. Life is reality, and I know what I have to do.

So somehow, with infinite strength and self control, she drew away from him and got to her feet. 'Thank you,' she said weakly. 'I shall be all right now. By the time I've walked home I shall be dry and warm through. Thank you, Daniel.'

She allowed herself a last look into his wondering eyes, as he stood so intently beside her.

'Alice,' his voice was very low and quiet, but throbbed with something that hurt her deeply. 'What is the matter? Why are you trying to get rid of me? What have I done?'

She sucked in a huge breath and tried hard

to find words that would deny her surging emotions. 'You haven't done anything, Daniel. It's just that—that . . .' Impossible to go on. Suddenly she choked, 'Oh, Daniel,' and threw her arms around his neck.

Like a miracle, all the unhappiness faded and she smiled into his bewildered face. 'Kiss me again,' she breathed. And then, with an almost wild laugh, 'The gorse is in bloom—it's kissing time. So shall we share a last goodbye kiss, Daniel?'

His powerful arms were strong about her as they kissed, but it didn't feel like a goodbye kiss. It was surely just the beginning of something wonderful. Yet she found the strength to pull away after that timeless moment of pleasure and turn from him, knowing that she must escape as fast as she could. His hands clutched at her but somehow she broke free.

'Alice!' His voice was desperate and she turned for a last look.

'I belong here, Daniel, on the moor,' she said urgently. 'You must go back to London and your friends there.' She thought of Daisy and then had to swallow the lump in her throat before she could go on. 'Forget me. Please— let me go.'

'But . . .'

She ran. This time there was no featherbed to hinder her rushing feet. No gorse to remind her that it was, truly, kissing time. All she knew was that she loved him, but that she must go home and think things through and tell herself that she must be sensible. Hurt and wounded she might be, but common sense told her she was doing the right thing.

His voice echoed after her but she closed her ears, telling herself that escape was the only way forward. So she ran—and kept on running.

A LETTER OF LOVE

Alice was halfway home when Ruby, Peter's dog, appeared, running up to her and offering a welcome. She stopped for a moment to pat its head and then, troubled, looked around.

Peter must be somewhere near, and of all people she had no wish to meet him at the moment. But then he came out of the circle of the Dancing Stones, looking at her with a stem expression as he approached, and saying, 'So you've been out with that Daniel Wells again. Mrs Hext said she saw you and then he followed.' Uneasily, Alice heard a note of aggression in his voice as he continued. 'Really, Alice, have you no idea how to behave?'

It was too much. Alice felt an unfamiliar rage swirl through her. She glared at him.

'And have you no idea, Peter, of how

129

unfriendly you are being? As it happens I was out alone, down by the river, and unfortunately stepped into a featherbed—and then, thank goodness, Daniel happened to come along and rescued me.'

She saw surprise replace the unpleasant expression on his face, and went on, 'And now I'm on my way home—alone. I see no bad behaviour in that, do you?' She heard the sharpness in her voice and hoped that he would accept what she said and argue no more. But it was a vain hope.

'But it's strange, isn't it, that he should know where you were?' His voice had an unpleasantly sly tone. 'It sounds to me as if you had arranged to meet.' Now he was returning her frown, and Alice knew that all she could do was to get home very fast and shut Peter and his scheming thoughts out.

'Please let me pass,' she said frostily. 'My feet are cold and wet and I need to get home and change my shoes and my clothes. Goodbye, Peter.' She stepped out as fast as she could and had the relief of knowing he didn't follow her. She heard his voice calling Ruby, and was thankful for small mercies.

Thankfully, Gemma was too absorbed in the new blouse she was making to notice wet boots and stained clothes. Alice crept upstairs and changed into a dry petticoat and skirt and then took the damp things down to Nellie to be dried out. 'I don't want to make a fuss,

Nellie—please don't tell my father or Gemma that I got so wet. They would only worry next time I go out.'

The old woman winked and nodded. 'All right, Miss Alice. Your secret and mine. But leave they featherbeds alone next time. Probably those wicked pixies led you, I reckon.'

*　　*　　*

The following morning Alice was sitting by the window, working on her notes, when Gemma looked up from her sewing and said in a soft little voice, 'Are you in love with Daniel, Alice?'

Alice caught her breath. 'Of course not!' she said spontaneously, but then, meeting her young sister's understanding eyes, said very slowly, 'Why do you ask such a question? I've never said anything about loving him, have I?'

Gemma put down her needle and thought for a moment. Then she said, 'No, you haven't. But I'm beginning to realise what it's like to be in love myself, and so I was thinking about you, and it seemed to me that when you are so quiet and sad-looking that you must be thinking of Daniel and wishing he were here.'

Alice looked into the intent hazel eyes watching her and suddenly realised that young Gemma had grown up overnight. She had met a man she could love, and so she understood more about life's pleasures and inevitable sorrows.

Alice knew she must go halfway to meet this new Gemma, so she said carefully, 'Yes, I do care for Daniel, but he's promised to someone else in London where his life is. And so I am trying to stop thinking about him.'

Gemma nodded, and began stitching again. But after a few seconds' pause, she looked up and asked, 'Is your heart broken, Alice?'

What could she say? Alice took a deep breath, blinked away the tears that now abruptly filled her eyes, and said unevenly, 'I hope not, Gemma. Certainly it's not a very happy heart at the moment. But I'm trying to get over my sad feelings.'

They looked at each other. Then Gemma said more cheerfully, 'I expect you're looking forward to going to London and visiting Aunt Joanna? It will take your mind off things, won't it?'

Alice smiled. 'Yes, of course it will. So let's start planning, shall we?' And then she added tenderly, 'but thank you for thinking about me, Gemma—and I do hope that your Richard will come very soon.'

'If he doesn't, then I shall definitely be the one with the broken heart!' Gemma answered, but she was smiling, and then the two girls laughed together and Alice felt something good had happened between them.

The next day she was sitting again by the window, with her notebook on her lap when the doorbell sounded and Peter Fletcher was shown into the room. She thought he looked slightly uneasy, yet his smile was as fixed as usual, as he said, 'Alice, I've come on a delicate mission. I hope you'll hear me through before you reply. Now . . .'

At her gesture he sat down opposite her and cleared his throat. 'I fear I have something disturbing to tell you.' His smile died and he looked at her very intently. His pale blue eyes were narrow and she sensed they were full of some sort of concealed excitement.

She felt a quiver of fear. 'Whatever is it, Peter?'

His smile died and he sucked in a huge breath. 'You are being talked about in the village. Gossip is rife. I hear it wherever I go, in the post office, in the shop, even in the church hall—yes, everywhere.'

She put down her pencil and moved the notebook to the table beside her. 'What on earth do you mean? What am I supposed to have done?'

He frowned. 'As if you don't know! You and that man, Wells, have been behaving without proper restraint, being alone several times, and your reputation is now in danger.'

Alice felt numb. He had mentioned this

133

before, but she hadn't taken it seriously. Now as she sat there it came to her that Gemma must have chattered on about she and Daniel being alone together in his old house. Intuition followed, and she understood that Peter was ready to use this knowledge, true or untrue as it might be, to get her to agree to something. And then the truth dawned.

Of course she knew what that something might be.

At last she said quietly, 'I see. Thank you for telling me, although I find it hard to believe. Daniel Wells and I have been far from indiscreet, but I know how village gossip can grow once someone lights the kindling . . .' She stared at him, hoping that her words were having an effect and that he might feel guilty.

But no. He got to his feet, stepped towards her and said roughly, 'You have no right to suspect me of anything save doing my duty, Alice. Indeed, I am the one person on your side. And I have come here this morning to offer you my hand in marriage. You know that I love you and, you see, once we announce our engagement, gossip will at once die down and your reputation will once more be safe.' He held out his hand and she stared at it, unable to bring herself to reach out and accept the gesture.

What could she say? On the one hand she was scared of causing her father and his school immense trouble if the village thought her unworthy of continuing to teach their children.

On the other was the fact that the only man she loved was Daniel, and she knew that Peter would never become the loving husband she longed for. Yet her father had advised her to consider his proposal. And Daniel clearly had no real feeling for her, save that of gratitude for helping to heal his wounds.

Numbly she sought words. They came unsteadily. 'Thank you, Peter, for the offer you've just made, but—I don't love you.'

His hands snatched at hers and pulled her towards him. 'But you will, Alice, you will learn to do so. Come, say you'll marry me and we'll kiss and seal the bond between us. Oh, Alice, Alice . . .' He was close, his mouth seeking hers, when thankfully she found the strength to pull away.

'Peter, you must give me time to think A week or so—please let me go. Come back another day.'

She hated the touch of his hands on hers, his lips so warm and demanding, and hoped desperately that her plea might keep him away until she had time to really think things through. 'I'm going to London soon—in a day or so—but when I come back I'll give you my answer. Please, Peter, wait a little, will you?' Her voice was faint, but determined, and to her relief he stepped back, watching while she sank into her chair, before returning to his own, which he pulled closer to her.

'Very well,' he said grudgingly. 'I'll wait, but I think you know the sensible answer must be yes. I mean, think of your father and your half-sister—you don't want to hurt them with the shame of the loss of your reputation, do you?'

Alice shook her head, unable to say any more. Clouds suddenly darkened her thoughts and she had an awful feeling that the only way to go was to marry Peter. But wait, she had said, just wait . . .

And then his customary jolly, but fixed, smile returned as he took a paper out of his pocket and handed it to her. 'And here is a token of my good will, Alice. It comes with an offer to illustrate your flower and folklore book for you. This rough sketch will give you a good idea of my talent.'

She took the paper from him and looked at it, askance. It was a rough painting of a small man, dressed in green and wearing an absurd red cap. She shook her head. 'Thank you, but exactly what is this supposed to be?'

For a moment he frowned, but then the smile flashed out again. 'Why, a Dartmoor pixie, of course—one of those wicked little folk who probably led you into the featherbed yesterday! Surely you recognise him? Green and red, and very small? You're writing about pixies, I know—well here is one!'

She was at a loss to know what to say. It was kind of him to make the offer, but clearly he was not a real artist. This was a travesty

136

of a drawing, almost childlike and not at all suitable for her book which was serious, even possibly academic in its contents. But how could she say so without making him angry again?

'Thank you Peter, it's very kind of you to offer, but I don't think, I mean—well . . .' Words trailed off and she was left looking into his suddenly narrowed and piercing eyes.

'I see. Not good enough, I suppose. Well, Alice, as my wife you will have to accept certain things, and one is that I am determined to illustrate your book.' Again the smile flashed out, warningly, she thought. 'I expect you need time now to think about my offer—in fact, my two offers.' He rose, bowed and then added, 'I look forward to seeing you again soon, Alice—your father has asked me to arrange a visit to Vitifer mine for you to talk to my cousin, Jem, the healer and I will let you know when we can go. In a day or two, I expect. And then you will be off to London, and I shall expect a firm answer from you on your return.' Leaning forward, he stooped low and stared into her flinching eyes. 'Although I am pretty sure of it already.'

At the door he looked back and she saw on his plain face an expression which disturbed her even further. He looked sure of himself, and was now showing indications of his behaviour at school with pupils who did not always do as he ordered.

Yes, Peter was becoming a bully. Yet she knew that she might have to marry him.

* * *

Alice had told her father about Peter's proposal and had seen his slow, anxious smile as he said quietly, 'The decision can only be yours, my dear. And as for your reputation being tainted, I think that is most unlikely. I've heard nothing of it.'

He looked at her with loving eyes. 'Perhaps Peter has gone a step too far in his longing to have you for his own,' he admitted. 'But I hope you and he might get over these difficult feelings when he accompanies you and Gemma to Vitifer mine. I have had a message from him, and he has arranged that you will go tomorrow afternoon, to meet his cousin when he comes off shift at the mine, before he goes home. I am allowing him to take the pony trap which he will drive, and I hope the afternoon will restore some of the friendliness you used to feel for him, my dear.'

Alice bowed her head. She knew that her father still thought Peter was a good man and perhaps he was right. Perhaps it was just that Peter's dreams about marrying her made him unpleasant at times, but then she straightened her back and concentrated on the questions she intended to ask the healer when they visited the mine.

Arrangements had also been made for Alice and Gemma to travel to London to stay with their aunt on the day after the visit to the mine. Gemma, of course, was excited and, adding to the business of going to London, was the letter she had received from Richard Westbrook apologising for not calling as he had promised.

She waved his letter under Alice's nose and said gleefully, 'But he'll definitely call when he comes back to Dartmoor, which could be soon . . . so I shall just keep waiting, and hoping . . .' she went out of the room singing and Alice was left shaking her head even as she smiled, for Gemma in love was even more exuberant than normal.

And then, on the morning of the proposed visit to the mine, the postman brought a letter for Alice, a large brown envelope addressed in a firm black hand.

She opened it wonderingly and was even more surprised when out fell a thick sheet of paper with a drawing on it. At once she knew what it was—a lifelike spray of prickly Dartmoor gorse, brilliant yellow flowers on a stem studded with dark green spikes. Her heart began to beat very fast.

Looking over her shoulder, Gemma said, 'That's gorse, what a good picture. Who painted that?' and Alice could only smile. She saw that a note was attached to the picture, and the few words written there were clear and, oh, so welcome.

Alice.

Please forgive me for whatever. I have done to hurt you. Hurting you is the very last thing I would ever want to do, so I send you a small gift of remorse, asking for forgiveness.

You will recognise the spray of gorse and I ask you very humbly if you will think about allowing me to draw—and perhaps paint, now that my hand is healed—further flowers for your book. I am in London now, but hope to return home— to Dartmoor—sometime. Shall I see you there?

With very sincere thoughts,

Daniel.

Silently, Alice passed the drawing to her father, who nodded and returned it. 'So Mr Wells is showing himself to be highly talented—what a surprise. I wonder why we were not allowed to know this before?' He took off his spectacles and looked at her kindly. 'Perhaps, my dear, if you are both in London, you might even meet? Your aunt has a wide circle of friends, you know.'

But Gemma had snatched away the note that Alice now held, and was waving it about. 'Goodness! He's got another name—why, he might even be famous! Look!'

And there, printed at the top of the notepaper, were the extraordinary words:

Daniel Hesketh Wells. Artist in Landscape and Portraiture. 10 Jermyn Street, London.

Alice was wide-eyed and full of confusion.

140

What did it all mean? Why had he not told her his full name? And was that the reason for Tom's hesitation when they first met on the moor? Could it mean that he was a well-known artist? And was he really, one day, coming back to Dartmoor? Coming home, he had said.

In the middle of spreading her toast with marmalade, she closed her eyes and dared to hope that dreams might, even now, come true. But then Peter's ingratiating smile and steely blue eyes flew into her mind, and she heard him again proposing to her. His cold and clumsy way of showing his caring for her made a chill run through her. And then she knew that, even though Daniel had sent a warm note and the painting, he had said nothing about his intentions towards her.

The world grew very grey. She told herself she would probably marry Peter and, even if Daniel did one day return, by then it would all be too late.

*   *   *

The day of the visit to Vitifer mine dawned cloudy and with stinging squalls of rain and wind. In the morning Gemma started packing ready for the next day's journey to London and Alice had no time for any more thoughts because of the questions her sister was demanding answers to.

'Shall we take our best hats? Are we

141

likely to go to church on Sunday? And what about shoes—Aunt Jo won't make us walk everywhere, will she? I suppose you'll take your awful old boots, but really, Alice, you can't possibly wear them in London! What will everybody think of you? You'll look just like a country bumpkin.' And then, 'Oh dear I don't mean to hurt you, darling Alice, but really you do need some new smart clothes, you know.'

'Yes, I'm sure I do. And if it will stop you going on and on then I promise to do so. At least I'll buy a new hat because I know you dislike my old dark velour so much.'

Now Alice was thankful that she could smile as she, too, packed her valise, and thought that perhaps Gemma's chatter was a useful antidote to the dark thoughts which had pursued her through so many sleepless nights just lately. And this proposed visit to the mine was quite exciting—she had a list of questions to ask Jem Fletcher, the healer, and was looking forward to his answers.

Even being with Peter might have its rewards, for perhaps she could try and understand him a little better instead of just disliking him. Dressing in a cape and a winter hat, in case of more rain, Alice put her notebook and several pencils in her satchel and kept it firmly over her shoulder as Peter brought the trap around to the front gate and helped them both to climb into the front seat.

He showed himself to be a competent driver

as they drove up the lane and towards the one road over Dartmoor which would take them to the Warren House Inn, the hostelry close to Vitifer mine.

The clouds parted as he halted the trap outside the inn and called a boy to take the pony into shelter while he and the girls went into the taproom.

The famous fire which was never allowed to go out burned cheerily in the huge hearth and the landlord greeted them welcomingly. 'Come in, come in, don't want to be out in this weather, I'll be bound. What'll it be to drink, ladies? Ale, cider, or if you wish I'm sure my missus can make you some tea.'

Gemma, eyes twinkling, said 'I'd like a small glass of cider, please, landlord.' She caught Alice's surprised look, and added, 'but a very small glass.'

They sat down at a long bench beside the window which looked out over stretching moorland. While Peter was talking to the landlord. Alice turned her attention to the wonderful view.

The squalls of rain had blown away and now sunlight lit up the valley in which the miners worked the iron ore which lay deep beneath the moorland surface. She saw buildings of all sorts filling the valley, the glance of sunlight on running water, and the everlasting motion of huge water wheels.

She understood that the big chasms and

mounds were all part of the mining work, most of which was underground, and then allowed her glance to wander beyond the industrial waste of the mine, for the moorland stretched, unhindered in its beauty and primitive power, as far as her eye could see.

When the tray of tea, cider and glass of ale for Peter arrived, she smiled at the buxom woman who brought it and said, 'This is a remote spot, Mrs Hutchings. But I suppose the miners bring you company.'

'And business. They work so hard, out in all weathers, standing in water most of the day, so an hour here when the shift ends is what they needs and we're glad to supply it, poor souls.' Mrs Hutchins smiled, nodded and disappeared into her kitchen.

Peter was looking at his watch. 'Jem should be here quite soon. As it's the end of the week, he'll be walking home instead of spending his nights here in the barracks.' He pointed towards the window and Alice looked at the tall building in the valley.

'And where is home, Peter? Far away?'

'Couple of miles, but some come from much further. Walking to work and then a day in the mine must be hard.' Peter's smile grew. 'I prefer being a schoolmaster, myself.'

As they politely laughed, the door burst open and a shabbily-dressed man entered. His clothes were wet and patched with earth and his hat, pulled low over his face, was sodden and filthy. But the eyes that looked straight at Alice were bright and curious. He took off his hat, shook himself free of raindrops and walked towards them as they sat by the window.

'Hello, cousin Peter. And ladies, good day to you.'

Alice was at once taken by the quiet voice which had a ring to it that touched a chord inside her and she felt sure that she and Jem Fletcher would be talking about things that were important to them both.

Peter shook his cousin's hand and Alice smiled to herself as she saw Peter's expression of distaste as he then wiped his damp hand behind his back and said, 'Well, Jem, what'll it be? Ale, I expect?'

'Aye. A glass to gladden the heart and warm the cockles. For I've been down that shaft for the last eight hours.' Jem looked enquiringly at Alice as he put a hand on a chair and she nodded. He pulled it close to the table and sat down opposite her. 'You asked to see me, ma'am. Well, here I am. What do you want to know, then?'

She felt a spread of comfort as she looked into the bright grey-green eyes. 'I understand you are a healer, Mr Fletcher.'

'Aye, and I'm necessary hereabouts. Working underground for eight hours at a time in the wet makes for poor health, so I does what I can to help them as needs me.'

Alice drew her notebook from her satchel and smiled at him. 'Do you mind if I take notes, Mr Fletcher? I am hoping to publish a book about Dartmoor and its legends and flower remedies.'

As he paused, clearly uncertain, she added, 'I have some flower names and uses in this notebook, and stories about pixies and featherbeds . . . and I would so like to be able to tell people about the natural healing that people like you are able to do. Would you mind?'

'A book?' Jem raised a wispy eyebrow.

'Well written and beautifully illustrated,' cut in Peter, nodding at Alice and smiling his big grin.

Gemma leaned over the table, looking curiously into Jem's lined face. 'What sort of things do you heal, Mr Fletcher? Do tell us.'

'Well—' He took a long drink from the tankard of ale Mrs Hutchins had brought and then returned Gemma's smile. 'I stop bleeding, cure warts and ringworm, and brings health where I can . . .'

Gemma stared at him, her smile fading as she said slowly, 'And can you cure a broken heart, Mr Fletcher? Because that's really why my sister is here—I do hope you can help her . . .'

In the shocked silence that followed her words, Peter frowned, Alice caught her breath, and Jem Fletcher very slowly nodded, still

146

looking at her. He smiled, as he said quietly, 'I'll do me best. Now, ma'am, sit still and listen to what I'm gonna say.'

A MISSING ITEM

Alice sat as if in a trance. Gemma's shocking question rang around her mind, but slowly she found herself able to concentrate on Jem's quiet words. And after a few seconds her mind cleared and she smiled into the eyes watching her so intently. 'Please forgive my sister for such a question, Mr Fletcher. She means well, I know, but I had no idea of offering myself as a patient . . .'

The lined face softened. ''Tis you that needs the healing, ma'am. I can see it in yer pretty face. So just listen, will you?'

Alice nodded and because of the warmth of the smile, and the power in the grey eyes, was able to sit back and let all her worries and fears drift away. She became unaware of Peter, uncomfortably fidgeting at the end of the bench, and of Gemma who sat close to her, one hand on her arm.

Jem's voice was quiet and soft, the words falling like music into the expectant silence.

'To lift all sadness, all weariness, all maladies and to restore to health and hope, praise God may all things be.'

As he stopped speaking, Alice felt something moving inside her, something warm and strong, becoming stronger as it grew. All her emotions ran through her mind, but then retreated into the background, and in their place she felt a new strength. Thinking for a long moment, she smiled to herself. For now even hope was daring to show its head . . .

'Thank you, Mr Fletcher. I shall never forget what you have said. What you have done for me.'

Her smile was radiant, and he nodded back at her, saying quietly, 'But you have to wait, me dear. Charms take a while to work proper.'

And then he sat back in his chair, drank a final gulp of ale and said casually, 'And what else can I tell you for this book, then, ma'am? Charms to stop bleeding after a fight, or an accident—words that'll send warts away and ringworm, too. And even a few old words that do stop certain wicked men overlooking the cattle of their neighbours . . .' But he was smiling, and suddenly the atmosphere lightened. Obligingly he told Alice of other charms and ways of healing, and the time flew by.

Gemma's voice was high and excited. 'How marvellous! I wish you could teach me some of those magical words, Mr Fletcher!'

He looked at her with kindly eyes. 'Aye, I expect you do, maid, but magic comes from in yourself and not just old words. Try looking for

148

it and see what happens. And remember, it all starts with love.'

'I will—oh, I will. Thank you, Mr Fletcher.' Gemma's face was full of smiles and her eyes gleamed with excitement.

Alice thought it was time to bring things back to everyday reality so pulled her notebook from her satchel and took up a pencil. 'May I write it all down, Jem?'

'If it pleases you, ma'am, and now I must be on me way. "Tis a long road back home and clouds are comin' up again. So I'll wish you well and say goodbye to you all.'

Quickly Alice said, 'Jem, you have been so generous with your stories —please allow me to give you something in return.'

He shook his head, got up, returned his empty glass to the bar, and headed to the door. In the open doorway he turned, looked back at Alice and nodded. 'Most kind, ma'am, but healers don't ask for reward. If they do the gift leave them, see? I'm just glad if I've been of any help, and p'raps I'll see you again some time when things have changed for the better, eh?'

He gave her a last, memorable smile and she smiled back, understanding that he had just given her a powerful gift, not only to write up in the notebook, but on a personal level. Somehow he had known that of all things she needed was the promise of a good life and hope. But she must wait.

Through the window, she saw him trudging away down the road, disappearing into the mist which now blew in over the moor. She sighed, then, putting on her cape again and arranging the satchel over one shoulder, she turned to Gemma. 'We must be getting home before the storm breaks. Father will be worried about us.'

Peter said quickly and with his customary self importance, 'No need—I can get you back to Stonely in record time. We'll beat the rain.'

Outside, the pony was once again standing in the shafts of the trap, and Peter rewarded the boy for his pains. He turned to her as she stood beside him, ready to climb into the seat. 'Now, Alice, let me help you into the trap. You should take off that satchel, I think. It'll make you more comfortable as you sit beside Gemma. I'll put it here in the back, under the horse blanket. Ready now, are we? Then off we go.'

He was right. They beat the expected storm by a few minutes, dismounting from the trap as the first sheets of rain poured down.

In the house Gemma and Alice took off their hats and capes and invited Peter to stay and have something warm to drink before walking back to his home lower down in the village, but he wouldn't stay.

'Must get back. Never mind the rain—I'll be home in two or three minutes. I hope you both enjoyed your meeting with cousin Jem? A bit of a rough diamond, of course, but he's well thought of on the moor.'

'Yes, he seems quite remarkable—and so wise.'

'Huh! Most of what he rambles on about is just old wives' tales. But still, you enjoyed it and that's all that matters. Goodbye now, Alice—and remember that I shall be waiting to see you after your return from London.' He looked at her with a meaningful expression, and then added, 'And I hope you have plenty of time for thought before you come back . . .'

Alice couldn't wait to get rid of him. Her head was full of new thoughts, of hopes and gratitude to Jem. She said, 'Yes, of course, Peter. I haven't forgotten our agreement. Well, goodbye now.'

She watched him nod, turn and go out of the house. The pony trap was driven around to the back of the cottage, and then she heard Peter's footsteps going down the street, on his way home. At last, she thought, at last I can think about what has just happened. And even what might happen, if Jem's words held any truth.

And then she was in the drawing room with Gemma sitting by the fire and chattering away to Mr Burnham about this amazing man in the wet clothes who had said such extraordinary things about magic and love, and of course, she was going to try and find the magic he talked about—it was her next great interest.

Mr Burnham nodded, smiled and listened, and then asked quietly that, if today was over, were his girls packed up and ready for the great journey to London, tomorrow? And that sent them upstairs, to make sure everything was indeed ready.

*   *   *

The train was slowing down as it arrived in Paddington station and Gemma was already up, pulling down their valises from the overhead rack. 'Alice, we've arrived—don't just sit there! Oh, but it's so crowded out there—I do hope Aunt Jo has come to meet us . . .'

And of course, she was there, tall and stately, elegantly dressed and with their father's kind brown eyes. 'My dears! How lovely to see you!' She hugged both girls, organised a porter for Gemma's many hatboxes and bags, and then they were climbing into a cab outside the station and travelling through crowded streets, towards her house in Kensington.

Gemma craned her neck to catch glimpses of the wonderful shops and stores lining the high street, but Alice was feeling out of her element. Memories of Peter and his bullying, of Daniel and the extraordinary new facts she now knew about him, even his warm kiss, were all churning about in her mind, despite her attempts to think of other things.

Even Jem Fletcher's words had faded. But, as the cab came to a halt outside Aunt Jo's house, Alice decided that, come what may, she must make the most of being here in this huge city. There would be fascinating places to see, shops, museums and galleries to explore and new people to meet, and perhaps, slowly, her life would improve.

Yes, she must put on a brave front. As Jem had said, wait for the charm to work . . . and in the meantime show her gratitude for Aunt Jo's kind invitation.

And so, when they were finally having tea in the drawing room, with its open french window overlooking the small but lovely oasis of green garden, she smiled at her aunt and said, 'It's very kind of you to invite us here, Aunt Jo. Gemma and I have been looking forward to coming for a long time,' and knew that she had turned the first difficult corner. Yes, it was necessary to be positive and to show how much she was enjoying herself.

Aunt Jo smiled her warm smile, stirred her tea and said quietly, 'And I'm sure the change of scene will do you both good.' She paused, then added, 'And especially you, Alice.'

They looked at each other and Alice sensed that her father must have told his sister some of the problems she was trying to deal with. No more was said, but Alice felt a new warmth creep through her.

Perhaps, she thought, she would be able to leave the sad memories behind her and concentrate on the happier present, and let Peter float into the future, or even, more hopefully, into the past, whispered a small voice at the back of her mind. But then she remembered that no-one could possibly predict what might happen at any time in this strange and mysterious world.

Aunt Jo was full of plans. 'I thought we might have an expedition to Kew Gardens to see the wonderful trees and flowers—there will be such beautiful colours at this time of year. And then perhaps go to an evening concert at the Queen's Hall. And what about looking at some art?'

Then she stopped, and laughed. 'While, of course, for Gemma a trip to Mr Selfridge's amazing department store is very important.' Alice saw how Gemma's eyes widened and shone and wondered vaguely whether, after this exciting London visit, her sister would ever settle again in quiet Dartmoor.

'But first,' went on Aunt Jo, 'I must give you both time to acclimatise yourselves! Dartmoor is so quiet and here it's all noise and crowds, as no doubt you've already discovered. So this evening I thought you could recover from all the rush and weariness of the journey and get your energy ready for venturing out tomorrow. Does that suit you, my dears?'

Of course it was just what they needed.

After tea was over Alice was quite content to sit there, looking into the garden and chatting with Aunt Jo, while Gemma at once picked up a magazine showing the season's new fashions.

They sat there, happily talking about family matters and the news of the day, until at last Aunt Jo looked at the clock on the mantelpiece and said, 'Well now, perhaps it's time for you to go upstairs. You'll find Debbie has unpacked for you so you can take time to freshen yourselves, ready for dinner. No need to dress this evening.' She led the way up the stairs. 'Gemma, you are in the little front room beside mine, and Alice, you shall have this back bedroom with its garden view.'

The girls thanked their thoughtful aunt and went their respective ways, Alice at once feeling pleasantly relaxed in the airy room allotted to her. She looked out of the window and saw the sinking sun decorating the bushes below with a golden sheen and at once thought of the moor and its glorious sunsets. But now, with determination and renewed strength, she was able to turn her thoughts to the happy days ahead that kind Aunt Jo had arranged. And slowly her imagination saw wonderful sights never before seen, while her mind envisaged different people, with minds full of interesting facts and suggestions.

Yes, London had so much to offer, and she was grateful for this opportunity of finding fresh amusements and ideas. Slowly and with a certain amount of amusement, she realised that the quiet little school teacher was suddenly ready to step out and discover the wide world that hid behind the primitive beauty and peace of Dartmoor.

When Gemma, a little later, ran into the room and bounced on the bed, Alice found it easy to smile. 'Shall I wear my lavender dress with the high collar?' asked Gemma. 'Or do you think this plain, rather dull blue would do—just for this evening? Tomorrow, of course, I shall get out my really smart clothes.'

Alice hid her smile, thinking as she did so, how lucky she was to have a sister who could always cheer her up. 'I think you should keep on the blue dress, Gemma. You look very pretty in it—it matches your eyes and yes, tomorrow you can definitely dress up a bit more.'

Gemma was pirouetting in front of the long mirror. She nodded and then, humming a little snatch of song, went back to her own room leaving Alice feeling brighter already. For London, she told herself, was waiting.

So forget Daniel, forget Peter, forget the gossiping village and just concentrate on the delights in store in the next few days.

At the end of the evening, Alice and Gemma were happy to go to bed early. It had been an exciting and wearisome day, with all the new experiences and sounds and sights. But before Alice undressed, she sat down by the window in her pleasant bedroom and thought back to the old, quiet life on Dartmoor. And then her book came to the front of her mind and, smiling, she reached for the satchel which had accompanied her to London.

She opened it, and then the smile died. No notebook. Feverishly, she turned out the contents of the satchel—pencils, the well-covered painting that Daniel had sent, and an eraser, but no sign of the notebook.

For a moment she sat there frozen, wondering, and then common sense took over. Of course she had forgotten to pack it safely away. It was probably in her valise or in her reticule, but further search produced nothing.

Then she thought back to the last time she had used the notebook—at the Warren House Inn, writing down the tales Jem Fletcher had told her. And then she had put it back in the satchel . . . well, perhaps Gemma had removed it for some reason. But why should she? Only one way to find out.

Knocking at Gemma's door she went in quickly, seeing her half-sister just about to brush her hair. 'Gemma, have you got my notebook?'

Gemma turned and stared. 'Your notebook? Of course not—why should I have it?' And then her mouth dropped opened. 'Goodness! Surely you haven't lost it?'

Alice felt herself tighten. 'No. I've probably

just put it somewhere—and I don't exactly remember where.'

They looked at each other, Gemma with the hairbrush still in mid-air, slowly coming down to start brushing her long golden hair. She thought for a moment, and then said, 'When did you have it last?' and Alice told her about writing down Jem's notes at the inn.

Gemma frowned at her reflection. 'And then it was time to go home and we went out into the rain, and Peter said . . .'

Suddenly it all came back, happening in front of Alice's eyes. 'Yes! He said give me the satchel because otherwise it will stick into Gemma's side when you sit together—and—'

'And he put it in the back of the trap under that smelly old horse blanket.'

Again their eyes met and Alice knew they were thinking the same thing. But it was too horrible to bring into the light. So she said carefully, 'I expect Father found it the next morning and took it into the house . . . it must be there, quite safe.'

Again Gemma frowned. 'But he would have said so when he drove us to the station to catch the train.' She put down the hairbrush and turned to look across the room. 'Alice. Are you thinking what I'm thinking?'

Alice swallowed the lump in her throat. 'I hope not. But I think I probably am.'

There was a hesitant pause, then Gemma said in a small, shocked voice, 'It's Peter, isn't it? You think that he—' Unable to say more, she shook her head.

Alice drew in a deep breath and then, slowly, said just what she thought, indeed, what by now she knew. 'He's taken it. Peter has taken my notebook. That's what I think.'

Gemma sighed. 'It certainly sounds like it. But why? Why on earth should he want your notebook?'

Alice shook her head wearily. 'Because it gives him a sort of power—well, almost a lever—to make me do what he wants me to do, I suppose.'

'You mean that he'll use the notebook to—to blackmail you?' Gemma was almost whispering, her eyes dark with distaste.

'Yes.'

'But—why should he want to do that, Alice?'

'Because he wants to marry me, that's why. And now I suppose the only chance I have of getting my notebook back will be for me to say *yes, Peter, I'll be your wife.*'

For a long moment neither of them said anything, until Gemma rose and put her arms around Alice. 'But you can't do that, can you? Because I know you're in love with Daniel.'

The moment stretched on until finally Alice smiled at her half-sister, and said quietly, 'We mustn't let all this spoil our night's sleep, dearest Gemma. We must be at our best tomorrow, so let's put Peter and his nasty

159

underhand ways behind us. Go to bed now, love, and I will too.'

Trying to lighten her voice in spite of her downcast feelings, Alice smiled brightly as she turned back to the door. 'You can dream of Richard Westbrook, and I—'

'You will dream of Daniel. I order you to do so, Alice Burnham! Goodnight now, and sleep well. Perhaps everything will be sorted out tomorrow. Father might write and say he has the notebook and then you can stop worrying.'

Alice nodded as cheerfully as she could. 'Of course. Goodnight, Gemma. And thank you for being so loving and kind.'

In her own bedroom she undressed and got into bed. But sleep eluded her. Peter and the notebook were in her dreams—but not Daniel.

ENJOYING LONDON

The next morning Alice awoke to unfamiliar noises—traffic, voices, even horses' hooves and iron wheels rattling along the street beside the house. It took her a few moments to realise where she was, and then all the old worries and pain came back. But Gemma was knocking on the door and came in, full of smiles and carrying a tray of tea.

'I met Debbie in the hall so I said I would bring it up to you. How did you sleep, Alice?'

160

And then, without waiting for an answer, she put the tray on the bedside table and sat down almost on top of Alice, eyes wide and smile radiant. 'I had the most wonderful dream! Do you know, Richard actually came here? I can't think how he knew where I was, but he smiled and looked at me with such a wonderful expression, that I knew at once we were in love!'

Alice sat up and poured her tea, instantly forgetting her sorry thoughts as she entered into her little sister's joy. 'How lovely for you. And what happened next?'

Gemma's smile faded. 'I woke up. Oh, why can't dreams go on for ever, I wonder?'

Alice sipped her tea and thought hard. 'Because life isn't a dream, it's real, and we have to work it out for ourselves! And now, if you will please get off my feet, I shall get up and get ready for breakfast.'

Gemma darted away to the door, smiling back over her shoulder. 'And after breakfast we are going to start doing all the wonderful things that dear Aunt Jo has arranged. I think I shall wear my second best walking suit, and perhaps trim my old hat with a new ribbon.'

Pouring herself a second cup of tea, Alice got out of bed and looked at the garden below. Sunlight touched the swaying leaves and a bumble bee droned past as she stood there.

Now she knew it was impossible to continue feeling unhappy and worried. The world was far too complex and astonishing a place to waste time on small fears and needless anxieties.

Perhaps Father had found the notebook— she decided to write to him at once after breakfast and ask him to set her mind at rest. And if not, well, then that would have to wait until she was home again, and Father would advise her how to deal with that wicked Peter Fletcher.

Dressing in an outdoor ensemble of pale blue banded merino wool that would be suitable for London wear, she felt happier and went downstairs to have breakfast with a smile on her face, and a sense of excitement buzzing inside her. After all, life wasn't all bad—and this was one of its better moments.

'Good morning, Aunt Jo.' She greeted her smiling aunt with a hug and felt again the warmth of the love being offered to her.

'I hope you slept well, Alice?'

A small pause as she stirred her porridge, and then said determinedly, 'Thank you, Aunt, I had a few awkward dreams, but this morning everything seems much brighter.'

Her aunt's eyes were understanding. 'Good girl. I think the future always manages to seem much more hopeful when one refuses to give in. Now, are you ready for a cup of coffee or do you prefer to wait and have it with your toast?'

The rest of the meal was enlivened with

Gemma's chatter and Alice's increasingly bright thoughts and remarks.

After breakfast she went upstairs to write to her father, and by the time she went downstairs again the letter was sealed and stamped, to be posted very soon and her mind was more settled.

Father must, of course, have the notebook. So foolish of her to worry. It was quite safe. And suddenly excitement built—London was waiting.

*   *   *

Yes, London was indeed waiting and appeared to be becoming impatient. Aunt Jo came into the sunny morning room where Alice sat looking at the newspaper and Gemma put the final stitches to the hem of her new blouse. Stopping in the doorway and smiling at them, she said, 'A visitor for you, girls.' Then she turned to the man following her and gestured for him to come into the room. 'Richard, of course Gemma has already met you, and this is my niece, Alice Burnham.'

Alice heard Gemma gasp and saw her half-sister suddenly drop her sewing, staring up at the handsome, blond young man who smiled at her, with a welcome in his bright blue eyes.

Gemma's voice was breathless. 'Richard! But I believed you to be still in Devon!'

'I was, Gemma, but London is my home.'

163

He looked down at her and his smile grew. 'I had to return here earlier than I expected. Business, you see. I was so sorry I hadn't the time to call on you and your family as I had hoped to do.'

He stood by Gemma's chair and Alice, entranced, watched the expression on both their faces.

Surprise and a growing excitement on Gemma's, and a hint of wanting to say something important, but knowing it was too early and incorrect to do so on his. She recognised the early signs of growing affection—reflections of her own feelings when she first met Daniel—and so understood exactly what was happening.

And then pain hit her with a cruel, well-aimed blow. She had told herself she had forgotten Daniel, but she realised now that one could never stop loving, try as one might, and this familiar feeling, spreading so strongly through her, was too strong to reject. Yes, she was missing Daniel and always would.

But Aunt Jo was speaking again. 'I must explain, girls—Richard is the son of a very old friend of mine. In fact, he's my godson.' She turned to Richard, and Alice watched them exchange smiles.

She felt there was real warmth and understanding between them and then thought briefly, and with a hint of dry amusement, that if Gemma and Richard were ever, sometime in the future, to declare their love, there would be no problem within the two families about them marrying.

Aunt Jo had seated herself, gesturing Richard to do the same. 'Now, girls,' she said brightly, 'Richard comes with a very interesting invitation.' She smiled at him. 'Tell them yourself, dear boy.'

'Well . . .' He hesitated, giving Alice time to look at him properly. Slight, perhaps a little taller than Gemma, with a mop of fair hair curling around his ears, clean shaven and blazing blue eyes, full of vitality and humour, he was certainly a handsome young man.

Alice watched him smiling at Gemma as he spoke and found herself agreeing with her sister that he definitely had great charm.

He cleared his throat. 'You see, my father owns the Westbrook Art Gallery in Bond Street, and he and one of his patrons—Lord Peters—will be awarding a prize in an event founded last year. This is a competition to find the most talented young artist in the country. Well, canvases have been arriving for days, all of them submitted for the prize and judging will take place at the end of the week.'

Gemma, obviously elated, was laughing and chattering, her eyes on Richard and her smile blooming as she said, 'If we come, does that mean we have to walk for hours around the gallery, staring at old paintings of foreign places and blowsy ladies wearing rather low

165

cut gowns?'

He grinned, eyes on her mobile face. 'Not if you don't want to. If you agree to come, Gemma,' turning he bowed at Aunt Jo and then at Alice, 'and all of you, of course—I shall make it my very pleasant duty to show you around. We can avoid the old paintings if you prefer, for there will be plenty of new ones, and I think these might be more appealing to you.'

'I would love to come!' Gemma turned shining eyes on her aunt. 'Aunt Jo, please say that we may go?'

Aunt Jo rose, smiling back at them as she walked towards the doorway. 'We will most certainly all go, child. And now I suggest that we reward Richard for his kind offer by having a cup of coffee or chocolate before we start out on our visit to Kew Gardens.'

Alice watched Richard bend forward to pick up Gemma's fallen sewing, heard his voice soften into near intimacy as he complimented her on the small stitches, saw her half-sister flush, and at once felt a terrible loss deep inside her. She knew that the attraction between the two of them was growing; oh, that hers for Daniel could continue as theirs would.

But then she found the strength to get up, saying in a steady voice, 'Excuse me if I go upstairs. I must collect my letter to Father so that I can post it while we are out.' At the door she looked back, giving her sister a warning look. 'And Gemma, don't chatter so much. I'm sure Mr Westbrook hasn't got the time to answer all your questions.'

But Gemma didn't hear. She merely looked into Richard's blue eyes and murmured that she hoped very much that he would accompany them to Kew.

It was quite a long journey to Richmond, but once there the little party, including Richard, who had said it would be a pleasure to accompany them, and then devoted himself to listening to Gemma's non-stop chatter and questions with what Alice thought was either devoted love or amazing patience, looked around them with growing interest.

The Gardens were looking beautiful, but the glorious radiance of the summer planting had faded. Yet the trees, with some of the most striking foliage, caught the late autumn sunshine, turning them into torches of fire, reminding Alice of Dartmoor sunsets.

*   *   *

After half an hour, Aunt Jo found a bench and sat down, saying firmly, 'This is enough walking for me at the moment. Alice, why don't you go into the Marianne North Gallery—just over there?' She pointed at a nearby building. 'It's full of oil paintings of the extraordinary plants that Miss North found when she was travelling in South America. I shall be happy to wait here.'

Alice was intrigued. 'Yes, Aunt, I'd like to do that.' She looked around her. 'But what about Gemma? I don't see her—where can she have got to?'

Aunt Jo smiled, her brown eyes shining with amusement. 'I shouldn't worry about Gemma. She's with Richard and I know he will look after her.'

Alice said quickly, 'I do hope she won't wear him out with her curiosity.'

Aunt Jo laughed. 'Not very likely. In my experience, young love puts up with all sorts of unconventional and strange things.'

'So you think—?' But Alice found herself thinking the same. Gemma and Richard were already finding each other extremely attractive, so time spent together could only enhance their feelings.

She sighed, thoughts ready to return her to her own personal emotions, but then she said firmly, 'If you're sure you are comfortable here, Aunt, I will certainly go and look at the gallery. I won't be long.'

Inside the quiet building she was immediately lost in wonder as she looked at the immense number of paintings of exotic plants, and it struck her at once that her proposed book—if she ever recovered the missing notebook—would benefit hugely in so many ways if she had illustrations of flowers. And that brought Daniel back into her mind—

although, truth to tell, he was never very far away.

Then abruptly she remembered—he had sent her the painting of gorse, safely tucked away in her valise back at Aunt Jo's house, and she hadn't answered him. Hadn't even thanked him. During the last few days, life had been so full . . . but how rude he must be thinking her.

She stood in a silent maze of inner shock. How terribly unappreciative she had been. Of course she must write a letter as soon as they returned to Kensington and send it off tonight—but then she paused. Where would Daniel be now? Then she recalled his note with the address on it—10 Jermyn Street, London—and realised with a flush of excitement that he wasn't very far away from her.

Returning home after the visit to the gardens, Gemma was still chattering on, only stopping when, back in Aunt Jo's house again, Richard said he must leave as his father was expecting him to help with work in the gallery.

Alice went upstairs to remove her hat and to write up her daily journal, but as she went, she noticed that Aunt Jo was talking to Richard in the hall below. And Gemma was beside them, eyes wide and for once—Alice smiled to herself—keeping quite silent.

She paused at the top of the stairs and kept looking, for something about their quiet voices made her wonder what they were talking about. Then she was surprised to see thee sets of eyes looking up at her, and wondered why her attention had been noticed. No-one said anything and so, rather embarrassed, she moved on towards her bedroom, but heard Aunt Jo say in her normal voice, 'Well, goodbye, Richard,' and his answer was that he would call with the carriage to collect them on Saturday morning about eleven o'clock.

And then she watched Gemma climbing the stairs slowly, looking back at the closed front door, showing no sign of her usually bright smile. Alice waited for her half-sister to go into her own bedroom and close the door. She had a feeling that Gemma was upset, and when she heard quiet sobs, she knocked and went in, to find Gemma lying on her bed, crying into her handkerchief.

Kneeling by the bed, Alice put her arms about Gemma. 'What's the matter, love?' she asked anxiously.

Gemma hiccupped. 'He's gone. Richard's gone away.'

'Well, of course he has. He has business matters to attend to, he told us so.'

'But,' another hiccup—'how can I be sure he just doesn't want to see me any more?'

Alice smiled, remembering the expression on Richard's face as he talked to Gemma earlier in the day. She had no doubt at all that he would be back. So she said lovingly, 'Stop worrying. Of course he'll come back.'

'But your Daniel didn't, and Jem's charm to heal your broken heart hasn't worked, has it? So perhaps Richard won't come back.' The words faded away. Gemma wiped her eyes and looked anxiously at Alice.

Alice's thoughts were difficult to control, but slowly she managed to find the right words to reassure Gemma. She smiled, and wiped the tangled hair away from her sister's sad little face.

'Aunt Jo and I saw the way he was looking at you. Of course you can be sure. Richard is different from Daniel.' She swallowed the lump in her throat and somehow managed to continue. 'Now, tidy yourself and come down to luncheon. And remember, we're going shopping this afternoon.'

That was enough to cheer Gemma up. She bounced off her bed and smiled again. 'And you must buy a new hat, Alice. Don't argue. Aunt Jo and I are quite determined that you must look your best for the rest of the week. And especially on Saturday.'

Returning to her own room, Alice wondered why Saturday was seemingly so important, but when she broached the subject over luncheon the only response she got was giggles from Gemma, and Aunt Jo simply changing the subject. Although Gemma did once grin and say, 'It's a surprise,' which was almost as bad as the continuing silence.

The afternoon was spent buying Alice's new

hat and a smart up-to-date walking costume for Gemma. The big store they visited actually had an elevator, which was highly exciting.

Gemma jumped on and then wobbled and wasn't sure whether to laugh or cry, but a shop worker stood at the top of the moving staircase and took her arm as she stepped off safely. And then, of course, all she could think about were the wonderful clothes on view. Tall mannequins filled the spacious rooms, with assistants ever ready to help and advise.

Alice was ushered into the hat department where she sat down on a velvet-covered stool in front of a huge mirror, with a very smartly dressed young lady beside her, offering hats of every conceivable style and colour.

'What shade is Madame looking for?' asked the girl and Alice had to think quickly.

On Saturday she would be wearing her best, but plain, dove-grey dress with the high neck and slightly puffed sleeves, falling down into tight cuffs at the wrist, the bodice decorated with dark wine red braid.

She hoped she wouldn't shock the waiting girl with her lack of knowledge about modern clothes, when she said quietly, 'Something elegant but not too stylish, and I think a dark red would be very nice.'

'And what does Madame think of this one? So very elegant, and with the roses dipping over Madame's brow, it would look so very, very chic.'

'I'm not sure that it's really me . . .' Alice turned her head from side to side, but the smile on the assistant's face gave her a new confidence. 'Do you think it suits me?'

'Madame, it suits you very well.' The girl's pert little face creased into a true smile and for a moment she forgot her cultured tones and said in a saucy London accent, 'And I bet no-one'll stop looking at you when you wear it.'

That did it. Alice left the department clutching a large bag and went in search of Gemma whom she found in a fitting room surrounded by a selection of costumes.

Gemma was fretting as she looked at herself in the long pier mirror. 'It's either this one or that one,' she pointed at another costume in the assistant's arms. This one was a black and white houndstooth costume, and that one was a beige gored skirt which developed into fullness at the back, and was topped by a smart jacket with big revers and elegant button decorations. It looked very well with Gemma's new blouse with the flowing scarf ties.

Alice sat down and readied herself for a long wait, but when Aunt Jo appeared, saying it was time to go home for tea, Gemma suddenly said, 'I'll take the beige one,' and then they were catching the omnibus back to Kensington and the excitement was over.

*   *   *

Alice sat in her bedroom early the next morning and wrote a letter of gratitude to Daniel. It was hard to know what to say—too much would perhaps encourage him to reply, not enough would not show how pleased she was with his offer to illustrate her book.

Finally, after much hard thought and several destroyed scribblings, she wrote:

Dear Daniel,

It was most kind of you to send me the beautiful drawing of the gorse, and to offer to draw—or even paint—other flowers for my book. I am extremely grateful, but feel —

Here she chewed her pen before being able to continue:

—that, owing to the fact that you live a very busy life in London, it would be unsuitable and an unnecessary extra labour for you to think further about my book. So once again, thank you for the generous offer which I regret that I cannot accept.

More chewing and painful visions of Daniel with Daisy. Until finally the pen descended, and she wrote:

I hope you keep well and that your hand and leg have quite recovered. Yours sincerely,

Alice Burnham.

Somehow, Alice managed to keep her thoughts from straying further, because the next few days were full of interest and pleasure.

A visit to Madame Tussaud's had them all fascinated, and full of wonder at the waxworks shown. And then Richard appeared—to Gemma's huge relief—on Thursday evening, to accompany them to the Queen's Hall to hear Fritz Kreisler, the famous violinist, play. Both she and Gemma were transported into a delightful world of music and pleasure.

And then, unexpectedly, after breakfast on Friday, Aunt Jo came into the garden where Alice was deadheading the bed of bright red geraniums and said, 'A visitor for you, my dear. Daniel Wells is here.'

AN UNDERSTANDING

Alice jumped up and felt herself go stiff with alarm. But the alarm was soon banished because then came the wonderful familiar, but forbidden, sensation of joy—Daniel was here! She was going to see him again—so forget the worries and fears—just for this moment she felt sheer happiness, and as he came through the open french window, she smiled, knowing her heart's pleasure was there for him to see.

But, although he said politely in his musical, low voice, 'Good morning, Alice, how nice to see you again,' she knew at once that something was wrong. Coldness spread through her and her smile died. Was it her letter? Had she offended him? She said nothing, but gestured to the deckchairs on the small terrace.

They sat down and looked at each other, until finally Daniel, on the edge of his chair, leaned forward and said quietly, in a deep voice that she could hardly hear, 'I've come to ask you the same old question, Alice. I was pleased to have your letter, but then what on earth have I done to make you feel we mustn't meet again?' His voice rose. 'You must tell me.'

What could she say? She sat stiffly for a few silent moments, seeking words, and then returning to the cruel fact that she knew he loved someone else. But this was part of his life, not hers. She couldn't speak about it. And then, unsteadily, words came.

'There is no reason, Daniel—of course you haven't offended me. But, our lives are so different, for I understand that you are a professional artist with many contacts here in London, while very soon I shall return to Dartmoor and my own quiet life as an ordinary village schoolteacher.'

She stopped, finally forcing herself to finish in a low, uneven voice, 'And Peter Fletcher has asked me to marry him. So you see, there is no future for us, and so it's best that we don't meet again.'

Daniel remained silent and she bowed her head, not wanting to see the expression which she had glimpsed spreading across his lean, taut face. Then she heard the chair scrape back, looked up to see him rising, looking down at her, unsmiling, his grey eyes shadowed and hurt, as he said gruffly, 'I see. Thank you for telling me. So this is goodbye, Alice?'

She could only nod, offer her hand without meeting that deep, penetrating glance. 'I'm sorry, Daniel ...'

'And so am I.' He stopped, took a step away and then turned back. 'But, Alice, if you should ever change your mind ...'

Suddenly it was all too much. She hunched herself into the depths of the chair, stared down at her hands, earth-stained from weeding, and managed to say in a shrill, uncharacteristic voice, 'Goodbye, Daniel. Goodbye!'

Silence, footsteps receding, and then voices in the hall, with the front door closing as if it were the end of a long drawn-out novel. Alice sat there until Aunt Jo appeared, looking anxious. 'My dear child, you look quite ill — what have you done?'

Alice slowly looked up, sucked in a deep breath and said in a broken voice, 'Under the circumstances I have done the only possible thing, Aunt. I have said goodbye to Daniel.'

'Yes, but—' Aunt Jo shook her head and then slowly retreated into the house, leaving Alice alone with her thoughts and her pain.

Somehow the time passed. Gemma went

shopping with Debbie, the maid, and came home full of glee, loaded with boxes. 'Oh, Alice, why didn't you come? The big shops are so exciting. Such gowns, and the hats—oh, just wonderful! But there, you did buy one the other afternoon, didn't you. And I know it will look splendid when we go to the gallery on Saturday.'

She pirouetted around the room, eyes sparkling. 'I shall wear my new beautiful beige walking costume with the honey-coloured blouse I made. What will you wear? Not that old blue thing you love so much, I hope?'

Alice realised that now that Gemma knew Richard hadn't forgotten her, she was full of dreams and plans. And then, even with her heart breaking, Alice knew she must somehow return to everyday life, and for once was grateful for her little sister's non-stop chatter.

After tea in her bedroom, she took out her dove-grey dress, held it up to her and then put on the new hat. The mirror showed an attractive reflection, and suddenly she was able to tell herself that life must go on, especially on Saturday, when she would please both Gemma and her aunt by wearing this handsome new hat with its large sweeping brim and decorations of dark red roses.

Perhaps, she thought, trying to smile at the foolish thought, if she looked somebody new, then she might even be able to step out into a new life.

Saturday dawned bright and warm and after breakfast Gemma pulled Alice upstairs. 'Richard is coming at eleven with the carriage,' she said excitedly. 'We mustn't be late. Do you think he'll like my new costume?' Going to the wardrobe, she took out the new garment and then found the hat she had been making for the last few days, and, in front of the mirror, settled it on her head.

Alice was able, after all, to smile again. 'Of course he will,' she said. 'You look lovely in it. And that hat is really quite beautiful—how clever you are.'

It was a small oyster-coloured toque, perched on top of Gemma's honey-fair hair and made with twists of golden and brown plaited velvet ribbon formed into rolls which fitted around her head. A spray of feathers fell over the final roll and was decorated with another spray and a bow of matching ribbon. Alice thought Gemma had never looked so pretty.

Half an hour later, when she had finished her own toilette, it was with a feeling of surprised pleasure that Alice heard her sister, looking her up and down, say critically, 'You look quite different, Alice. For all its plainness, that grey dress suits you, and that hat is most elegant. When . . .'

She stopped abruptly, grinned and said, 'Oh, never mind. Let's go down and wait in the garden, shall we? I don't want to sit down and

179

crease my new skirt. Well, I suppose I'll just have to keep walking about. But it won't be long before Richard comes.'

He arrived at one minute to eleven o'clock and after a whirl of excitement, collecting bags and wraps and umbrellas in case of rain, very soon the carriage was bowling along the crowded streets, releasing them eventually at the Westbrook Gallery entrance, where Richard conducted them into a spacious and beautifully-decorated foyer, and then on, into a back salon already thronged with groups of people.

Gemma looked around with shining eyes. 'Richard! It's so lovely here, but where are the pictures?'

He smiled. 'I'll take you through the different galleries, Gemma. Tell me what you would like to see—Italian cities, ladies in undress or some pretty landscapes?'

Gemma laughed. 'Let's see them all. Come on, Alice—and you, Aunt Jo.'

And then they were off, walking slowly through huge, spacious rooms with their walls covered with amazing pictures and portraits.

By the time they had exhausted all the galleries in the large building, Richard led them into a final room, saying, 'And these are the competition entries. All portraits and all by contemporary artists. Which one do you think will win?'

Gemma stopped by a portrait of a fine-looking older man standing beside his thoroughbred horse in a green, unruffled pasture, surrounded by distant hills and lit by the gleam of a river. 'He is so handsome,' she said. 'I'd like this one to win.'

But Alice, slowly inspecting all the entries, finally halted by the portrait of a very beautiful young woman in a garden, leaning against a pergola covered with white roses.

The woman had a heart-shaped face, and her dark, lustrous hair hung over one shoulder, elegantly decorating the simple white gown she wore. It was a face that instantly told Alice here was a kind-hearted woman, someone who understood the trials of life, and who would doubtless give all her love to one deserving man. She wondered who the woman might be, and which artist had depicted her so perfectly that it seemed the character was about to step out of the frame.

But then raised voices told Alice that it was time to return to the flower-decorated salon. People were gathering and looking expectantly at the raised dais at the end of the big room. She joined Gemma and Aunt Jo and watched while Richard, excusing himself, disappeared through a wide open door behind the dais.

Through it, after a slight pause, came two elderly men, following by Richard, leading a gathering of men and women who looked around them with, Alice thought, some expressions of desperation, before settling themselves on the small gilt chairs provided behind the dais.

Then she understood. The man with the pepper and salt hair and matching beard bore a likeness to Richard—this was Mr Westbrook himself. And the other upright, beaming and clean-shaven man with a military bearing, had notes in his hand and so must be the patron of the competition.

Gemma turned to her, whispering excitedly, 'This must be the prizewinning. And, oh, Alice, look over there . . .' she nodded towards the middle of the group of waiting artists, and Alice's heart began to beat fast enough to take flight.

So this was the surprise that Gemma and Aunt Jo had been secretly planning—they knew Daniel would be here.

She saw him. He wore a dark blue suit, his linen was crisply white, and she thought his face still bore the healthy, sun-kissed tan he had acquired in his days on Dartmoor. He was looking around and she hoped madly, foolishly, that he would see her. Gone were all her inhibitions in an instant, gone the knowledge that Peter Fletcher awaited her answer in Stonely—gone was everything save her love for this one man.

And yes, he had seen her. She saw his mouth slowly lift into that wonderful smile which had captured her heart when they first met. Slowly, he nodded at her, and for that one moment Alice knew supreme happiness. It didn't matter what might happen next, for now, in this glorious precise second in time, she and Daniel were one.

And then all her emotions were swept away as Lord Peters began his speech. He welcomed everyone to the Westbrook Gallery. 'The one place in London where art reigns supreme, thanks to its owner and his son.' He then went on to explain just what the occasion was.

Alice glanced at Gemma, who was spellbound, eyes shining and fixed on Richard. For that moment she understood that her little sister was as much in love with him as she herself was with Daniel—something they could share for the rest of their lives, perhaps, whatever might happen in the unpredictable future.

Lord Peters was continuing to speak. 'This has been an extremely difficult task, choosing which of the many excellent canvases submitted should win Mr Westbrook's annual prize.'

He stopped and nodded his head, and Alice watched his face fill with pleasure as he went on. 'But one portrait alone stood out—and both Mr Westbrook and I are unanimous about this—and that is the portrait of Lady Daisy Moreton.' He paused, looked over his spectacles at the enthralled audience, who gave a quiet hum of approval, and then said slowly, 'and the artist is Daniel Hesketh Wells, our prizewinner for this year.'

Suddenly, all Alice's glowing joy was swept away. Daisy. So Daniel had painted Daisy, and it was so clear that he had felt love for her as he picked up his brush and began to paint.

As he had told her when they visited his old home on Dartmoor, Daisy had been a childhood friend. Beautiful and generous-hearted, he had called her and then said how good it was to meet her again and renew the old friendship.

And now, clearly, that old friendship had become love. Alice knew she only had to look again at the portrait to see the love in Daisy's eyes.

The clapping and the exclamations of admiration, the sudden hum of excited conversation, ran around Alice's churning mind and she groped to find the nearest chair.

She wished with all her heart that she could run and hide. This was all too much to bear.

Her head whirled and she feared she might faint, but then Aunt Jo's arms were supporting her, helping her unobtrusively to move away to the open window behind them.

Here Alice stood, breathing deeply, not really hearing all that went on behind her until Gemma came to her side and whispered, 'Oh, Alice, Daniel has won! Isn't it splendid? And look—he's coming over . . .'

Somehow Alice managed to control her emotions and gather her strength, and then turned in time to find Daniel at her side. He was looking at her with what she realised was deep concern in his eyes. 'Alice, are you pleased? I do hope so.'

She struggled for words, hoping she could convey her pleasure and admiration without revealing those deeper, painful feelings that were churning inside her.

At last, she said, quite steadily, 'Of course I'm pleased, Daniel. I congratulate you. And the portrait is very beautiful—Lady Daisy looks so real that I felt she might step out into the room.'

He nodded and smiled, but she saw from his expression that he was hoping for something more.

And although she was still feeling highly emotional, she managed to say what she thought he expected to hear. 'Daniel, from the way you have painted her, and her own wonderful warmth and grace, I feel sure you and Lady Daisy will be very happy together.'

She watched his smile die, saw a frown darkening his eyes, and then, to her complete amazement, saw him take a deep breath and then let it out in a great burst of laughter. Suddenly his smile returned, this time full of understanding and amusement.

'What? You think that Daisy and I are—?' He leaned forward, took her hand as he said urgently, 'Come over here, Alice. I want you to meet her.'

At his side, she walked across the room, now full of chattering groups of artists and their families and friends, with many faces turning to look at Daniel and smiling, offering their congratulations. He led her to three people talking. Lord Peters, an unknown man and the beautiful woman of the portrait.

'Excuse me, Lord Peters, for interrupting, but I want Daisy to meet Alice. It's very important.'

At once the tall man nodded, raising a wry eyebrow. 'Go ahead, young man Today is your day, you know.'

Daniel held Alice's hand in a strong, warm grasp and said, 'Daisy, this is my good friend, Alice Burnham, who has helped to heal my wounds.' He turned to look at Alice. 'And this is Daisy Moreton.' Briefly he paused, smiling at the man who stood beside them, watching. 'And this is Daisy's husband, Sir Gerald Moreton.'

Alice felt her head swimming. She could say nothing, but suddenly deep inside her a glow of warmth began to thaw her frozen feelings. Heartfelt joy filled her now. So Daisy was married!

All her unhappiness and heartbreak had had no real basis. Daniel didn't love Daisy, as she had thought. And then, out of the blue, came Jem Fletcher's words about waiting for the charm to work, and then she heard again how Daniel had asked her, only a few days

186

ago, to tell him if she had changed her mind.

Sensibly then, Alice knew she must claim the happiness that she had thought was not for her. She looked at Daniel, smiled into his expectant eyes, and said, very clearly, 'Daniel, you said that if I changed my mind . . .'

He nodded, smiling. 'I did.'

Still she had to make sure. 'But did you really mean it?'

Carefully, excusing them from Lord Peters and the Moretons, Daniel drew her apart from the crowds into a quiet corner and then said, very steadily, his voice deep and full, 'I never meant anything so much in all my life, Alice. Oh my darling, don't send me away again — just tell me that you care.'

She leaned into his arms, sheltered by a conveniently-long hanging curtain. 'I do care. Of course I do! I always have done. Oh, Daniel, I care so much!'

And then Aunt Jo was signalling that it was time to leave the gallery as the carriage was waiting, and Gemma was saying goodbye to Richard and waving back to him as Alice joined them, walking back to the entrance.

At her side Daniel held her hand and said, in a low voice, as everyone started making their farewells, 'I shall call later in the day, my darling. And then we must make plans for our future together.'

Alice looked into his bright, silver-grey eyes and saw happiness there. She knew then that

187

whatever happened in the future—Peter flew through her mind, the missing notebook, the gossip in Stonely village—she could face all of it now, with Daniel at her side.

He came after tea, politely asking Aunt Jo permission to talk to Alice, and together they told her of their love.

Aunt Jo was delighted. 'My dears! This is wonderful news. Alice, you must telegraph to your father.'

Daniel's voice was strong and full of pleasure. 'I shall return to my cousin Dauntsey's house, Miss Burnham, and then call on your brother to ask for Alice's hand in marriage.'

'Which I'm quite sure he will grant you, Daniel!' Aunt Jo laughed. 'He couldn't possibly refuse, could he? After all, having a famous son-in-law who is clearly head over heels with his daughter is as much as any father can expect!'

'I shall travel to Devon as soon as I can once I have made all the arrangements for things that have cropped up as a result of winning the prize—a few commissions, and such like—I think it will only take a few days.'

Aunt Jo was thoughtful. 'Alice, you and Gemma will no doubt travel home tomorrow—and I shall be alone again.' Her tone was light, but she glanced at Gemma, whose face had suddenly clouded. And then she added, 'but perhaps Gemma would like to stay on a little longer. Wouldn't you, my dear?'

Alice was surprised to see her sister's face slowly grow very serious as Gemma said, after a pause, 'Thank you, Aunt, I would love to stay, but . . .' She looked at Alice and went on slowly, clearly thinking hard and choosing her words with care, 'but I would rather go home and be with Alice because I know she has all sorts of problems to sort out. I mean, I could help her find her notebook and perhaps when Peter calls I could, well, just be there with her.'

Alice's emotions threatened to overflow. Never before had Gemma put anyone before her own needs, and now—now she was not only offering her help, but even turning down the opportunity of seeing Richard again in London.

Newly aware of other's feelings, because of her own happiness, Alice understood that her little sister was putting filial love ahead of her growing love for handsome Richard Westbrook.

It was difficult to speak, but she managed to find the right words, unsteady though they were. 'Thank you, Gemma, and I shall certainly need your help when we get home. And perhaps Richard will be visiting the Dauntseys again before long.'

And then they were all talking about Daniel's wonderful achievement, until he reluctantly said he must leave. He had to meet someone who was very keen to commission a portrait of his small daughter.

'Well, goodbye for the moment then, Alice.' He looked at her with longing, and she wanted to throw herself into his arms. And then dear Aunt Jo came to the rescue.

'Go and see Daniel off, Alice. But don't stay too long, it gets cold in the evening.'

Alice understood the unsaid suggestion, and smiled gratefully at her aunt. 'We'll just say goodnight, and then I'll come back,' she promised.

Outside the front door the tall garden shrubs and the growing dusky light promised seclusion. With Daniel's arm encircling her, she lifted her face to look into his glowing eyes. 'I love you so much,' she whispered, and felt his arms grow tighter.

He bent his head and found her lips, and she knew, at long last, that Jem's charm had truly worked. Happiness for them both. What more could they ever ask?

He released her reluctantly, put on his hat and said lovingly, 'and so it's goodbye until I come back to Dartmoor, my darling. Until then I shall think of you, dream of you—but now must go. So goodnight, sweetheart.'

Alice watched him stride away down the darkening street and then returned to the warmth of Aunt Jo's drawing room.

She sat dreaming by the fire, hoping that her father, having by now received the telegram announcing her arrival tomorrow, would understood the love she and Daniel shared. And then, of course, little by little, the dark shadows tried to return.

Where was her notebook? What would she say to Peter Fletcher? And was the village truly affronted by her so-called outrageous behaviour?

But, as Aunt Jo called her into supper, Alice felt a new strength filling her. With Daniel at her side—his arms about her, his lips warm and demanding on hers—she could face whatever life was threatening to throw in her way.

'I'LL BE DOWN FOR THE WEDDING'

On the station platform, Alice hugged Aunt Jo. 'You knew all the time about Daniel, didn't you, dear Aunt? And you planned the great surprise—thank you, with all my heart.' Then, saying their goodbyes was a sad business, both Alice and Gemma repeating how much they had enjoyed themselves, while Aunt Jo kept smiling, and even laughingly called out to them as the train slowly departed from Paddington station—'I'll be down for the wedding—or should I say weddings?'

Gemma settled herself down in one corner of the compartment with Alice facing her. They looked at each other and smiled and

191

Alice said, 'Dare I ask if Richard has said he will see you again soon?'

Gemma nodded, her eyes sparkling 'He wrote me a note which arrived this morning saying he will try to visit the Dauntseys when he can. It might be a week, he said—so I shall hope all the time until he comes.' She leaned forward and took Alice's hands. 'Being in love is wonderful! Is this how you feel about Daniel?'

Alice thought for a moment and then smiled back, as she said, 'I feel as if my life has taken wings, and I can't believe I'm so lucky to have found Daniel, whom I know is the only man for me.'

Gemma sat back again. 'Not luck, Alice— magic. Remember the charm Jem Fletcher gave you? He said it might take time to work— and now it has. Will you go and thank him, I wonder?'

Alice thought back to Jem's words. *To lift all sadness, all weariness, all maladies, and to restore to health and hope*, and smiled as she said, 'Yes, I will. And perhaps Daniel will come with me, but I don't know what I can give Jem. He said healers can take no payment or their gift leaves them. What do you think?'

'Hmm. Have to really think about that.' A pause and then she added, 'What about a pretty bunch of all your old healing flowers? Would they come in handy for him, do you think?'

192

Alice said at once, 'A wonderful idea, Gemma! Thank you—yes, of course, that's what I shall take him.'

'That's settled, then. Good.' She looked out of the window, and then exclaimed, 'Goodbye, London! Alice, we're almost in the country again—and oh, I'm so looking forward to being home in Devon.'

'I never thought I'd hear you say that, Gemma. You always said the country was so boring.'

'But then I'd never been to London and seen the shops, and travelled in a hansom cab, had I? Never gone to concerts and art galleries and met a most marvellous man who I think has fallen in love with me! Yes, of course I shall enjoy being at home with you and Father.' She giggled and added quickly, 'But only for a little while. And then I shall go to London again! After all, Aunt Jo has invited me, hasn't she?'

Both girls had plenty to think about then, and by the time they had eaten the picnic Aunt Jo had provided, they were arriving at Exeter station and looking for the trap which Mr Burnham had telegraphed that he would arrange to collect them.

It waited outside the station yard, and within minutes the pleasant young driver stowed their valises in the back, and they settled themselves with rugs and shawls ready for the journey to Dartmoor.

Alice relished every mile the pony covered, for here was familiar country, every landmark filling her with pleasure and once again making her appreciate her love for the green lanes, high hills and rushing rivers. And then, the temperature dropping and their rugs being tucked more securely about their feet, they were rattling over open moorland.

The heather was over, just brown bushes now, with bleached moorgrass and gorse providing the only colour. Sheep lay in the shelter of the road verges to avoid the wind, and ponies grazed in groups.

The tors were covered in cloud, and Alice recognised the approaching winter look of the moor. Different from summer sunshine and fast-moving shadows, but almost more beautiful in its primitive loneliness.

And then her thoughts returned to her notebook with all the stories and remedies she had written into it. Wherever it was, she must find it. Some of the stories ran through her mind, and then . . .

'When the gorse is in flower, 'tis kissing time.'

Alice smiled to herself, and knew she would never forget Mrs Spreyton's advice, which then reminded her of the beautiful painting of gorse which Daniel had sent her, now safely packed in her valise. And then, of course, Peter came into her mind, and her smile died. Being at Stonely, home with Father and Gemma, was going to be wonderful, but so many problems awaited her there.

*   *   *

Reaching Apple Cottage was as pleasurable as both girls had expected, with Father and Nellie coming to the front door and welcoming them both. Hugs and kisses brought them into the warmth of the drawing room where a fire crackled in the hearth and the table was laid with Nellie's Devonshire splits and—of course—a pot of clotted cream. There was so much to talk about, so many tales to tell, news to exchange, and then—

As the tea cups emptied, Alice found the courage to turn to her father and ask carefully, 'Father, what news of my notebook? Have you found it?'

Mr Burnham's face tightened and he smiled gravely at Alice as he replied slowly, 'My dear, I'm afraid the notebook was not in the trap as you had suggested.' He paused, 'But I do know where it is.' He smiled.

His dark eyes looked anxiously at her, saw her face drop, and then he went on carefully, 'I fear that what I have to tell you won't please you. You see, Peter Fletcher has been to see me and has told me that the notebook is in his possession.' He stopped.

Alice tensed, caught between relief that at least the notebook was safe, and unease about Peter having it. At last she found words. 'Thank goodness we know where it is, Father.' A weak smile crossed her face, as she tried to reassure him. 'But what did Peter say about it?'

Mr Burnham sat well back in his chair and raised his head a few inches. Alice recognised the stance from dealings with difficult pupils at school, and felt her heart start to race.

'Peter Fletcher,' said her father crisply, 'is showing himself in a new light which I find quite unacceptable. For one thing he tells me it is high time I retired and he became head teacher of my school. For another . . .' he rapped fingers on the table and his voice rose, 'He has told me that you will only have the notebook returned to you if you agree to many him.'

Silence tightened the room, Gemma staring with disbelief at her father, and Alice feeling all her old problems rushing back into her life. 'Of course,' went on Mr Burnham, 'I replied by telling him that blackmail is a chargeable offence within the realm and that if he continued practising it I would consult my family solicitor.'

Alice took a deep breath. 'And what did he say to that, Father?'

'He stormed out of the house, refusing to listen further.'

She hardly dared ask, but forced out the words. 'And taking my notebook with him?'

'I'm afraid so, Alice, my dear.'

They looked at each other understandingly and then Gemma said firmly, 'How horrid of him. I think I shall go and tell him what I think of him! How dare he treat you, like this, Alice.'

Alice sighed. 'He dares because he has high ambitions, Gemma. To be headmaster and to marry me. So perhaps I shall just have to accept that my notebook won't come back.'

She stopped, realising what that meant, and then continued, in a small voice, 'So I shall have to start doing all that work again.'

'Certainly not,' Mr Burnham exploded. 'The wretched man must be made to see his errors and to stop all his demands. I shall see Frank Courtney tomorrow when I go into town and start proceedings against him.' He looked at Alice with fire in his dark eyes. 'And in the meanwhile, take no notice of anything he has said, my dear. All will be well in the end. Indeed, I intend to make sure that it will.'

Then the old warmth returned, and they deliberately changed the subject. But Alice found it hard to sleep that night. Her thoughts went around her head in heavy succession, until suddenly Jem Fletcher's words came to her.

To lift all sadness, all weariness, all maladies . . . and on the edge of sleep, she told herself, with new lightness of heart, that Peter was simply one of those unwanted maladies. And that he would be lifted soon—how, she was not

197

sure, but as part of Jem's charm had already worked, she knew the rest would follow. She was certain about that.

AN UNKIND DISPLAY

The next morning she knew what to do. Asking Gemma to accompany her, they left the cottage after Mr Burnham had gone into town to see his solicitor and walked down through the village towards the church and the school. As they walked, Alice said, 'Now Gemma, please tell me if any of the cottagers are looking at me with horror—they might well do so.'

Gemma stared at her. 'Why? What have you done?'

Alice found she could laugh. 'Behaving, so Peter said, in an uninhibited and shocking way, walking alone with Daniel and visiting his ruined house with him. Which, of course, is mostly your fault, for telling Peter, but please watch out for nasty stares.'

Gemma said nothing, but her wide eyes and frown said a lot. They passed Mrs Davy's cottage and Alice was relieved to see the good old woman smiling out of her window and waving.

Then they went past the post office where the postmaster looked out of the open door and called, 'Good to see you back, ladies—the village didn't seem the same without you,' and they both waved to him.

'There, you see,' Gemma said quickly, 'what nonsense Peter was talking—just another example of his nasty ways.'

It was a huge relief to Alice to understand that all this so-called gossip had been purely in Peter's malevolent mind. But it still didn't resolve the problem of his demanding the headship of the village school, or the return of her notebook. Once they had completed the circuit of the village with smiles and waves from many cottage occupants, they returned home to find Nellie waiting with a message.

'Boy from Dauntsey's called with this letter, Miss Alice.'

Alice took off her coat and went into the morning room to read it. Large, firm black handwriting and Daniel's signature at the end. A smile helped overtake shaking fingers as she opened the folded paper and read.

My darling.

I could wait no longer, all the business matters here in London must wait. I am here at Churchill House and will be calling on your father tomorrow morning at ten o'clock. I hope he will be ready to receive me—and then you and I can start making plans for our future.

Dearest Alice, I will be with you in less than twenty-four hours, which can't go quickly enough. Wait for me,

Daniel.

She dropped the letter into her lap and leaned back in the chair. What did Peter and the notebook and the school problem matter? Daniel would be here tomorrow—and after that they could think about their future . . . the rest of the day passed in radiant dreams and plans about happiness and charms coming true. Alice closed her eyes and lost herself in a new, wonderful world—magic, indeed!

In the morning it was Peter who called first, directly after breakfast, demanding to see Alice and then approaching her with his fixed, rather sinister smile. 'So you're back! I heard the gossip about your return in the village and so here I am, to have your answer, dear Alice. You recall, I'm sure, that you promised me you would think while you were in London, and so I am waiting.'

Alice, alone with him in the morning room, stood up and walked to the window, turning to look back at him after she had composed her thoughts. Words, then, came quickly and easily.

'Yes, I have thought, Peter, and I have to tell you that I hope to marry Daniel Wells, so must give you my answer of no.' She felt very sure of herself and watched Peter's face go red and then pale again, patches of colour remaining in his thin cheeks.

'But this is ridiculous,' he stormed, voice rising and filling the room. 'Your father knows that you have to marry me because—'

She cut in sharply. 'Because you have stolen my notebook and think you can blackmail me? I understand that, Peter, but nothing you can do or say will make me change my mind. If you insist on keeping the book, then I shall simply start my work all over again. I won't let you stop me.'

Footsteps in the hall outside the room made them both keep silent for a moment, staring at each other. Mr Burnham entered, approaching Peter with a dark frown on his face and waving a document at him.

'I must ask you to leave my house, Peter Fletcher,' he said coldly. 'I have to inform you that my solicitor is charging you with intended blackmail.' The paper he held was flapped in Peter's astounded face. 'And moreover, you have upset my daughter, Alice, with many unpleasant incidents and suggestions. Lastly, I am discharging you from your position as deputy headmaster of our village school.'

Alice watched Peter gasp and then prepare to argue. But Mr Burnham was a match for him. 'Don't bother with false explanations or making more threats, Peter. Just go, if you please—and don't ever come back.' He strode into the hall, opened the front door and stood beside it.

Peter seemed at a loss. His colour receded to a grey pallor, and Alice saw his hands shaking with anger as he followed Mr

Burnham, passing him and slowly walking into the garden. There, he turned and shouted, 'You may think you've got rid of me, but remember, I still have Alice's famous notebook, and I can assure you that she will never see it again!'

As the last words left his lips, a trap drew up outside, and Alice saw Daniel jumping down, tethering the cob, and then standing at the gate, watching as Peter raged and fumed and Mr Burnham simply turned away and disappeared into the house.

Alice flew into the garden to warn Daniel, but there was no need. He clearly had understood that Peter was being ejected, and that he was taking it badly. Perhaps it was the last sentence about Alice's notebook that made Daniel walk into the garden and then shut the gate behind him. He stood in front of Peter, looking at him with cold eyes, and said in a hard voice, 'Give me the notebook, Fletcher. You have no right to it.'

Peter, surprised by this new attack, backed a few steps away, then sneered into Daniel's face, 'I have every right. She said she would marry me.'

It was too much for Alice. 'That's untrue and you know it,' she cried, moving swiftly towards Daniel and holding out her hand to him.

Daniel grasped it firmly, giving her his warm smile, but she heard a chill in his deep voice.

'Go back into the house, Alice, this is between Peter and me. I don't want you involved.'

Slowly she obeyed, returning to the open front door where Gemma now stood, eyes aghast at the scene being enacted in front of her. Alice put her arm around her sister's shoulder and felt her warmth giving her strength. She could do nothing but stand there and watch and hope that Peter would give in without resorting to violence.

But she saw his right arm lift and strike at Daniel's chest. 'If you want the wretched little book then you'll have to come and take it from me—see, it's here, in my pocket . . .' He waved the notebook in the air as Daniel stumbled and then found his balance again.

Gemma cuddled closer to Alice. 'Oh, they're not going to fight, are they?'

Alice whispered, 'I don't know,' and watched as Daniel stepped forward and aimed a blow at Peter's chin. A small voice inside her said, *that's the hand you helped heal,* and she wondered if there had been a reason for finding the right remedy to give Daniel such strength. But then all her thoughts vanished as she saw the two men struggling, with Peter gasping and shouting and Daniel narrowing his eyes and endeavouring to get hold of the notebook.

And then she saw his hand grasp it. He backed away at once, holding the book safely and standing and watching as Peter clumsily backed out of the garden, turning to look at Alice and then retreating down the road without further speech.

Only then did she realise that it was all over. The book was safe in Daniel's keeping, Peter was being charged with blackmail and he would have to accept his discharge from the village school. Gemma was laughing and cheering as she watched Peter's humiliating defeat, but Alice found tears in her eyes as she went into Daniel's waiting arms. 'Thank you,' she said shakily. 'Thank you, dear Daniel . . .'

And then Mr Burnham appeared in the open doorway. 'Good morning, Wells,' he said, and Alice knew there was warmth and a hint of amusement in the formal greeting. 'So you've got rid of the fly in the ointment? Well done. I don't think we shall have any more trouble with him

'And now, I gather you want to speak to me? Of course, I can't possibly imagine about what, but come in, come in, dear fellow. We'll have a few moments alone in my study, shall we?' He turned to Alice and Gemma, who watched and listened intently. 'And you young ladies can think about preparing some coffee while we have our little chat. We'll be back in the morning room very shortly.'

Daniel gave Alice a last smile as he followed Mr Burnham into the study, and she was left wondering if the last part of her problems was about to be resolved. But what if father didn't

204

agree to her marrying Daniel? Ridiculous to worry, of course, but she was glad to have something to do to distract her thoughts, and so helped Gemma with the making of the coffee very willingly.

*   *   *

Ten minutes later they all sat around the fire in the morning room and Alice knew she had no need to worry ever any more. Mr Burnham stirred sugar into his coffee and said in a jocular voice, 'Alice, my love, I have given Daniel my willing permission to ask you to marry him. He's proved himself to be a courageous and honest fellow—and indeed, a talented one with a good future—and I feel will always consider you and do his best to make you happy.' His smile was wide. 'So now all that remains, is for him to actually propose . . . why not show him around the garden? But wear a shawl—even love can't stop the cold winds, you know.'

Alice and Daniel left the room amid laughter and went through the house and into the back garden. Alone in the little gazebo at the end of the lawn, they faced each other and Daniel took her into his arms. 'Darling Alice,' he said huskily, 'I have no words to tell you how much I love you—only a few, and they are—please will you many me?'

She lifted her head to look into his face and

felt all her love centring on one word. 'Yes,' she said unevenly, and then no more was needed, for he was kissing her and she knew again, and this time for good, the excitement and thrill of true love and happiness.

'YOU HAVE TO FINISH YOUR BOOK'

Of course, they both had to come down to earth before too long, and back in the morning room plans began to be made. Mr Burnham said sadly, 'So not only will I be losing Peter Fletcher, but also my best teacher, Alice. I shall have to start looking around for replacements before the term starts again.' He looked at Daniel, now sipping coffee and also holding Alice's hand in his. 'Where do you propose to live, Daniel? In London, or somewhere a little nearer?'

'I shall keep on my studio in Jermyn Street, sir,' Daniel said, smiling at Alice. 'But my plan is to bring my old home at Chagford into a liveable state and settle there. If Alice agrees, of course . . .'

'There's nothing I should like better,' she whispered, seeing his silvery eyes light up. 'And perhaps I can help with the work—I could do some painting and wallpapering, perhaps, and, and . . .'

Daniel laughed. 'All in good time. There's a

lot to do before that can happen. And anyway, you have to finish your book.'

He produced the notebook from his pocket and put it on her lap. 'And I have to paint your pictures . . .'

Mr Burnham cleared his throat, looking thoughtful. 'Perhaps you might consider staying here, while you work on the old house, Daniel? We have an unused guest room . . .'

And so it was arranged. While Daniel worked at Chagford during the day, employing several local men to help, he painted flower pictures in the evenings.

Alice revised her book and decided it was full enough to offer to a publishing house. Gemma, of course, dreamed of Richard and waited impatiently for the letters which arrived every few days. Life seemed ecstatically happy, and one day Alice knew there was a final task to be done.

When she and Daniel were strolling on the moor one Sunday afternoon, she said, 'I would like to go back to Vitifer mine, and give Jem Fletcher a small thank you for working his charm on me.'

'What charm was that? You never told me . . .' Daniel pressed her arm and smiled into her eyes.

'A charm to lift a broken heart,' she said simply. 'And it worked.'

They went to Warren House Inn on the following Friday afternoon and watched while the mineworkers ended their shifts and began the homeward walk.

'There he is,' said Alice at the window. 'Daniel, please ask him to come in for a minute . . .'

Jem Fletcher seemed surprised at the request, but came in and looked amiably at Alice.

'You wanted to see me, ma'am,?'

'I do, Mr Fletcher, indeed I do. I must tell you how grateful I am for the charm you gave to me, which has indeed worked. Thank you with all my heart.'

'What was that, then? Which charm do you mean?'

'To lift all sadness, all weariness, all maladies and to restore to health and hope,' she said softly, and offered him the small bunch of healing flowers she had collected especially for this thanksgiving.

He looked at her, then at the flowers, and smiled. 'Healing herbs,' he mused and nodded. 'Thank you, ma'am, I'll make good use of 'em, but remember, it wasn't my words that healed you, no, 'twas good old moorland magic.'

Just for a moment silence grew between them, and then Jem turned away. 'I'll be going home now. And I don't think as how you'll need me again, maid, but if you should, well, I'll be there.' He walked to the door, gave them a last smile and then disappeared into the growing mist of the moorland evening.

Daniel and Alice drove back to Stonely slowly, renewing their love for the moorland landscape as they did so. 'The tors are almost invisible as the mist comes down,' said Alice softly. 'But we have the rest of our lives to see them again in the sunshine, haven't we, my love?'

Daniel bent his head and kissed her, and it seemed that, just for that moment, a small magical ray of light shafted through the oncoming mist, lighting their way home.